A Different Matter

"The wolf, Sergeant, is a most inefficient hunter. That is why it is so vital to the balance of nature. A wolf does not kill a healthy animal. It cannot. It is neither fast enough or strong enough. The wolf takes the aging, the sick, the malformed—and strengthens the species on which it preys."

"What do you think about werewolves?" the sergeant asked. He blushed as he spoke, expecting her to laugh at him.

She didn't laugh. Her eyes gleamed, but not with laughter. "That," she said, "is a different matter. . ."

WOLF TRACKS

David Case

BELMONT TOWER BOOKS ● **NEW YORK CITY**

A BELMONT TOWER BOOK

Published by

Tower Publications, Inc.
Two Park Avenue
New York, N.Y. 10016

Copyright © 1980 by Tower Publications, Inc.

Chapter One

When the farmer came upon the track of the timber wolf he paused to reflect for he hadn't seen a wolf track on his land for a long time. Now they were coming back. It was no longer legal to shoot them and they were coming back. It figured, thought the farmer. They were tough, wolves were. He had never lost any stock to a wolf but he knew men who had. He went home to get his gun. It was his land and maybe it was against the law but what the hell. It wasn't much of a law. He came back with his gun and began to track the wolf without much passion. If he found it on his land he was going to shoot it but he wasn't going to chase it very far. He simply felt obligated to make a mild effort. But when he found the wolf it was already dead. The legs were sticking straight up in the air, grey and stiff as fenceposts and the body was horribly mangled. The farmer looked down at the dead wolf and rubbed his neck. He actually felt sorry for the wolf. What the hell could do that to a timberwolf? he wondered.

Chapter Two

Like a Stone Age monolith, the CN Tower rose above the neon and plastic of downtown Toronto. It always reminded Sandy Dawson of the robots in *War Of the Worlds* and she was looking up at it as she walked down Yonge Street. There was a full moon, pale behind tormented clouds, and the tower flashed with lights. Eerie, was what Sandy thought. The lights ran up and down. She wasn't at all sure that she approved of the tower. She figured it was a useless structure, built just so Canada could have a taller *thing* than the United States. On the other hand, she loved H.G. Wells and liked to imagine bloated Martians at the top of the tower, so her feelings were ambivalent. She felt no ambivalence about the other new buildings, though; she thought it wicked that fine old houses had been razed in favor of oblongs of glass and steel that looked more like aviaries than buildings. Sandy was no fan of progress and not at all materialistic, which was just as well because she had no money. She was wandering the streets, just passing time. She was seventeen years old.

It was a chilly evening with grim, writhing clouds. Sandy's feet were cold and she blew on her hands from time to time. When she came to the

Eton Center she turned in and walked down the underground concourse, figuring it would be warmer there. It was like a whole different city, she thought; shops and restaurants and gardens under the earth, where people might lead their whole lives and never see the light of day. She wondered it anyone was doing that, leading a totally subterranean existence? Mole people. Like the Morlochs in *The Time Machine*. She really did like Wells. But the concourse was deserted at this hour and she saw no one, Morloch or human.

She strolled through the empty, echoing cavern, heels clicking on the tiles, stopping to window shop from time to time. She wished she had some money. It was all well and good to renouce the Capitalist Society but she sure would have liked a new pair of shoes.

It was warmer under the streets, out of the wind, but soon Sandy began to feel oppressed by the mass of buildings above her. She felt pressed down into solitude. Scorning a capitalist society, the girl was still social. She wanted new shoes, too. She walked on past a big fountain and turned up another flight of stairs.

A figure stepped out from the shadows at the top and started down the stairs, bulky in a heavy coat, hat drawn low over his brow. There was a curious lurch to his step as he descended, as if he were not used to stairways. Sandy figured he was probably drunk, some hopeless wretch seeking shelter. She hoped he wouldn't ask her for money. She kept her eyes lowered.

Then she heard him breathing.

It was a labored, ponderous sound, as if he were straining under a great burden. Sandy looked up.

Only three steps separated them now and she looked up from an angle, under the brim of his hat. She saw him.

Sandy's face went blank.

The figure lurched closer and Sandy took a step back. Her eyes widened and her mouth contorted. His hand came up and Sandy spun around and ran back down the stairs. At the bottom she looked back. He was still descending, coming faster now. Sandy ran along the empty corridor and he was running, too. His footfalls echoed hers. He was still lurching, she could tell that by the uneven sound of his feet, but it was an efficient lurch, like a lumbering bear; she knew he was gaining on her.

One of her heels broke off and spun away like a quoit.

Oh no, she thought; oh no.

She darted around the corner and came to a set of firedoors. His shadow loomed up in front of her, on the doors; his bulk blocked the passageway. She was panting now and she could still hear his breath; it billowed after her. Sandy yanked at the handle and found the doors locked. For an absurd instant, she was indignant—firedoors weren't supposed to be locked!

She pulled futilely at the handle and she was watching his shadow as it spread out and up on the doors. His arms were up. Her mouth was open. She screamed at the doors.

Then she turned to face him.

His hat had slipped back now; she could see his face and she screamed again. He reached for her. She was too terrified to move, she just stood there screaming right into his face as he lowered that terrible face to hers . . . .

Chapter Three

Ike Clanton, burly, fierce, and bearded, was a cynical man who nevertheless looked consistently on the bright side of things, a strange combination that suited his condition, for Ike had no legs. He'd lost them years before when, trying to hop a freight train while drunk, he slipped under the wheels. Ike had a little wooden platform with rollers and he managed to get around pretty well with his big torso strapped to the platform and his gnarled hands stroking the pavement. He could wheel about sharply and nip and tuck and he thought himself lucky to be so nimble. Having no legs wasn't really so bad. He wasn't expected to work, for one thing, and while working itself wasn't so bad Ike was old now and, had he worked, he would have been forced to retire and he would have hated that, since he didn't have enough money to retire to Florida. People took pity on him, too, and were generous when he panhandled. And—maybe best of all—when you didn't have any legs blind guys didn't keep bugging you to help them across the street.

Ike Clanton, both surely and cheerful, was wheeling his way home past the Eton Center on his nifty platform. Ike bitterly resented the Center. It was, he thought, just like society to scoop out the bowels of the earth and not equip the entrances with ramps, never giving a thought for legless fellows. He would have liked to roll down in there and get warm, for it was truly a chilly night. The wind was whipping around through the streets, tossing a tattered newspaper along the gutter like a reflection of the clouds it was shredding above. Ike figured that if he could fit a sail to his platform, he could blow home.

When he heard the girl scream, the first time, he thought it was the wind.

He halted abruptly and reversed up against the wall, lighted a cigarette, holding it cupped in his big, rough hands. His face glowed ferociously in the flare of the match. He inhaled deeply, warming his powerful lungs against the chill. He smoked a lot and figured that cancer was scared of him.

Then he heard the second scream and it was definitely human, the way it was prolonged and then broken off short. The sound didn't taper like the wind. Broken was the word.

Ike scowled and looked about, turning his massive head as if his neck was a swivel. Sounded like a woman, he thought. None of his business. But he stayed where he was, backed up to the wall, smoking hard.

After a while he heard footsteps dragging on the stairs and he saw the bulky figure come out of the underground concourse. Clouds had drifted across the moon, filtering the light. He could not see clearly. But there was something about the figure, something menacing, and Ike cupped his cigarette so the glow didn't show. He held his breath. The shape moved past him, not too close, and Ike stayed where he was.

The figure drew abreast of him. Just then, the wind ripped a cloud apart and a shaft of moonlight fell directly on the passing figure for a moment. Ike had glimpsed the man's face. Ike thought it was a man's face. He still held his breath and shielded the

10

cigarette. Maybe it was a man's face. Maybe it was just the way the moonlight hit it. Sure, maybe.

Ike was no coward.

But Ike was glad that he didn't have legs so he didn't have to be brave . . . .

Chapter Four

The cop on the desk was yawning.

It had been a slow night and he was bored but he guessed that was better than lots of work. His name was Billings. When he yawned he took his hat off. It was an automatic gesture. He lifted his hat off his head and his mouth yawned open; he put the hat back on and his jaw closed. When the man walked in he was halfway between; he clapped his hat on and watched the man approach the desk. He was middle-aged and wore spectacles and Billings thought he looked nervous or timid or reluctant. Maybe he looked ashamed. Billings figured he had been rolled by a hooker.

"Yes sir?" Billings said.

The man was hesitant. He said, "I just saw . . . a remarkable thing." He paused and when Billings said nothing, added, "I don't know if I should report it . . . or . . ."

Or stuff it? Billings thought.

"If you'll tell me what this . . . er . . . remarkable thing was . . .?"

"If it had been Hallowe'en . . ." the man said, and then he grinned sheepishly. "Well, I don't

11

want you to think I'm crazy."

Billings sighed. He had his pencil out and squared a form on the desk in front of him. Usually, when a guy said he didn't want you to think he was crazy, there was a pretty good chance he was nutty as a fruitcake. Billings studied him. He didn't look crazy. He was wearing a suit and a necktie and he looked nervous or maybe worried but he didn't look crazy. People usually looked worried when they came to the police station. Billings figured he had better help the guy out.

"Name, sir?"

He wrote it down.

"Address?"

"Well . . . I'm staying at the King Edward hotel."

Billings wrote that down. He wasn't interested enough to ask for the man's home address.

"Now, then, sir . . ."

"Well, I just saw an animal wearing clothing."

Oh boy! Billings thought.

"An animal," he said. "Wearing clothing."

"That's right. An ape, maybe. Well, I don't think it was an ape, exactly. Some upright animal."

Billings moved his pencil around but he didn't know what to write yet; he said, "Where was this, sir?"

"Outside the hotel. Let me tell you . . ."

"Yes, why don't you do that?"

"I'd just parked my car and when I got out I saw this thing in the shadows of the building. It was . . . well, it was pretty damned scary. I mean, it wasn't like some joke animal, some performing animal dressed up like a man . . . and it wasn't some man wearing a mask, either. It was scary. Rumbling."

"Rumbling?"

"Growling. In the throat. I had just got out of the car and I stood there. I still had the door open. I was looking at this thing . . . and it was looking back at me. Its eyes . . . glowed. It was dark there, it was standing in the shadows, and yet its eyes glowed. Like a cat's eyes, gathering whatever light there was reflecting it back—like that."

"I see," Billings said.

"Well, I got back in the car. I was . . . really frightened. I closed the door and locked it and I was going to drive off, but then this thing moved away. I waited for awhile to make sure it was gone. Then I came around here."

The man paused and shrugged. Billings knew he should ask him some questions. The man was waiting to be questioned. But what the hell did you ask?

"How big was this thing?" he asked.

"My size . . . the size of a man."

"You say it was wearing clothes. What do you mean?"

"Why, clothing. A coat . . . hat . . . clothing."

"Well-dressed, was it? Was it breaking any laws? Loitering, would you say it was, sir?"

The man tensed and stiffened.

Billings thought maybe he had been a bit too sarcastic. Sometimes these nuts reported you for being sarcastic and then you got hell for it.

He said, "Could it have been some promotion stunt? Publicity for a movie, something like that? Sometimes they do things like that. I remember, *Planet of the Apes* was playing here, what did they do but send people out in monkey suits. The whole damned city was filled with people in monkey suits. They got machine guns, they're getting on the busses . . . what I mean is, could it have been something like that?"

"Perhaps that was it," the man said.

He was obviously annoyed now. Billings regretted his sarcasm. He was there to serve and protect, not to mock the public. But sometimes you just couldn't help it. The guy didn't look so worried now; not so nervous. He just looked annoyed. A little disturbed, maybe.

Billings said, "Well, I'll fill out a report, sir."

But the man said, "Perhaps I shouldn't have troubled you. Perhaps I was mistaken. I'll be staying at the hotel for a few days, just in case . . . well, I just thought I should report it."

"Yes, you were right to report it," Billings said. I hope he doesn't report me, he thought. "Thank you, sir. We'll look into it."

The man nodded. He waited a moment, then turned and walked out. He walked okay; he was sober. Billings took his hat off to scratch his head and as soon as the hat came off, he yawned automatically. Jeez, he thought, the things that you get . . .

Chapter Five

The bars were closing but there were plenty of all-night diners and dance clubs and Yonge Street was still vibrant and loud when Harland James came walking down it, his thick spectacles flashing with reflected neon. He was looking around. He was a middle-aged man with flat planes to his face and might have been handsome but for the eyeglasses which, magnifying his eyes, made him look perpetually startled. He figured he probably looked like a rubbernecking hick with his head tilting around and the idea amused him. Harland was no tourist. But he hadn't been in Toronto in some time and he was surprised at how much the city had changed. Well, he thought, everything changes. How long has it been since I was last here?

He couldn't remember.

He knew he hadn't been there since Paul fled to Canada and then he grinned, amused at himself for thinking in those terms. I'm getting old, he thought.

He knew he was putting things off.

He'd come as soon as he got Paul's disturbed—and disturbing—letter, but now that he was here he was nervous about seeing the boy. Still, he couldn't put it off forever and he thought he had better find a telephone and call first—that would be easier than showing up unannounced. The best place to find a telephone was in a bar, he thought, and he could use a drink before he called. It was a hell of a thing when you needed a drink before you phoned your own son.

But the bars were closing.

Customers were leaving under protest and the lights were going off. He saw one young man swinging a beer bottle like a semaphore as he staggered out; another tried to fight his way back upstream to the entrance, like a salmon eager to spawn. Harland looked at his wristwatch and was surprised to see how late it was. The evening had

15

slipped right by; time passes and everything changes.

Well, it was too late to telephone now. He was relieved. And, suddenly, he was exhausted. As if his body ran by clockwork, keyed by the hands of his watch, he felt his energy ebb away.

He deciced to go back to the hotel and go to bed.

He walked back down the street. It was darker down that way and when he came to the entrance to the underground concourse he paused for a moment. He had heard that they'd built an underground level below the city. But he didn't go down. He knew he would feel claustrophobic in a place like that and he felt sorry for the people who worked down there—they must go to their jobs like Christians to the catacombs, he thought.

Chapter Six

Milly McGee had a terrible hangover and was in a foul mood as she stomped down the street in her platform soles. She'd had a date the night before and the guy had obviously intended to get her drunk so he could have his way with her. They'd gone on a pub crawl and both of them had drunk plenty. And then the guy had vomited and passed out and hadn't had his way with her at all. Now Milly was furious because she had a hangover for nothing. There was nothing worse than a hangover, she thought, especially when you had to go to work. Milly worked in a florist shop in the underground concourse and had to be there early to open the place. She knew the heavy smell of flowers would make her sick. She thought she might quit her job; if the boss gave her a hard time, she was going to quit on the spot and that was that.

She went down the stairs, thinking just what she would say to her boss if he so much as blinked at her and when she came to the side corridor she walked right on past. Then she turned back, frowning. Something had caught her eye, something crumpled up against the fire doors.

Milly looked at it.

Then she knew there were things worse than hangovers.

Chapter Seven

Well, he'd seen murders before and he reckoned he was pretty well hardened to violence but he didn't like the look of this one at all. His name was Steve LaRoche and he was the staff sergeant handling the homocide team from Jarvis Street. He was forty-two years old, lean, gray-eyed. He stood with his arms folded across his chest.

Sergeant Greene was standing beside him. Greene was young and round-faced and slightly rumpled. He kept looking at the body and then looking at LaRoche and it was obvious that he was pretty badly shaken. LaRoche didn't blame him. It wasn't pretty. The girl had been pretty, he could still tell that much, and somehow that made it uglier, because she wasn't pretty now.

The identification officer was talking to the criminal investigator, keeping his voice soft in the echoing chamber. Two police artists were working and they didn't like the subject matter. One had been sick. He'd studied art and wanted to be a painter. Now he was drawing corpses. Jesus. Presently he was sick again.

Greene said, "Christ, it looks like—" he paused as he heard his voice bounce from the walls, louder than he'd intended. More softly, he said, "It looks like she was savaged by some sort of animal."

He didn't like looking at the body and he couldn't look away from it; his eyes were pinned as if somehow his gaze had got stuck in that congealed blood. There were some thick grey hairs in the soft red wounds.

LaRoche said, "Seen a few floaters in my time; never saw one quite like this."

"Floaters?" Greene said. "Floaters?"

"Yeah. Dead 'uns."

Greene stared at him.

LaRoche shrugged; said, "Dead 'uns float, got it?"

"Aw, hell, Steve. Don't talk that way. You been watching too much television, talk like that."

He glanced at the body again and the skin rippled at his hairline. A few of the thick grey hairs were sticking straight up from the open flesh, like spikes; the others were embedded like primordial insects trapped in red amber.

Greene said, "She was just a young girl, Steve."

"Sure she was. But she's floating now."

"You're a callous bastard, Steve."

LaRoche's mouth twitched. For a moment, Greene thought he was going to grin. But he said,

"That's as may be. The thing is, I'm objective, Joe. That's the thing." His voice was deeper than Greene's. When it hit the walls it didn't bounce, it went flat. "A thing like this, if we don't think objectively about it, maybe we don't do our job. And what we want to do, we want to get this guy before he kills someone else. So this one, she's dead already, she's a floater. Right?"

"Aw, hell." Greene aborted a gesture. "You figure it was a guy, huh? Looks more like an animal to me. The way she's all . . . chewed . . ."

Greene's jaw worked as if, unconsciously, he was imitating that chewing. Then he realized what he was doing and stopped. LaRoche was right. There was no room for sentiment or imagination in a thing like this and the cold bastard was right. But she had been young and pretty and hell . . .

One of the uniformed cops wandered back from where he'd been cordoning off the corridor. He looked at the body and made a muffled sound. He had a daughter about that age.

"Sure it was a guy," LaaRoche said.

"What about those hairs?"

LaRoche shrugged.

"I think it was an animal."

"Wht you want to do? Leave the body here as bait?"

Greene blanched. He shook his head.

"We won't speculate," LaRoche said. "We'll let the pathologist tell us what killed her."

"Well . . . say it was a man, Steve. If it was . . . you figure he'll kill again, huh?"

"Oh, sure," said LaRoche, absently.

Greene didn't want to see another body like that one.

LaRoche said, "Unless we get him first."

Greene grinned. LaRoche shrugged again. It was the work of a man, all right, he was thinking. It was too bestial for an animal. Then he told himself to cut out thoughts like that.

Chapter Eight

Gus Tyson was the daytime bartender at the White Rose and he had just opened the place. There was one customer at the bar. Gus fancied himself a good judge of character and often tried to guess the occupation of strangers, as if a man's job symbolized his essence. He had come pretty close on the first customer of the day. Wash McCoy had been a professional boxer, fighting out of Detroit, but he'd never been more than a club fighter and when he retired from the ring he moved to Toronto. Wash was black and had heard there were less prejudice north of the border. Quite a few of his friends from Detroit had also moved to Toronto, but they were mostly pimps. Wash had taken a job in a meat packing plant. Gus had figured him for an entertainer. That was pretty close.

Gus was serving Wash a second beer when another customer walked in. The newcomer stood just inside the door, looking around uncertainly, as if not sure he wanted to come in. Gus looked at him, wondering what he did for a living. It was hard to say. Sometimes you could hit it straight off and sometimes you couldn't. This guy might have been anything. He had big eyes.

It was Harland James and he was looking for the telephone. He spooted it on the wall at the back. Then he went up to the bar. He still wanted a drink or two before he phoned his son. He felt nervous and lonely. Normally, Harland hated crowds but that morning he would have preferred a crowded bar, even a noisy bar, and he was thinking that it was funny how a man could be lonely in a big city, with people all around him. He was never lonely when he was alone. He could be off in the mountains somewhere, no one for miles around, and not be lonely at all. That stuff about no man being an island—that was just crap, he thought. You were alone inside your skin.

He took a stool next to Wash McCoy.

They hadn't had bars in Canada the last time he was there. You had to sit at tables and have burly waiters sling draft beers at you, two by two. That had been lonely, all right. Paul had sounded damned lonely in his letter. Times change. The telephone was right there on the wall but he was going to have a drink first, damned if he wasn't.

Gus wandered down the bar, slapping at the surface with a rag. He thought maybe the guy was a queer, the way he sat next to McCoy with the whole bar empty. He didn't care, he just thought it. He thought maybe McCoy would wallop the guy if he tried any funny stuff. He stopped opposite Harland.

He said, "Yeah?"

Harland thought for a moment.

"Shot of rye . . . beer chaser."

Gus thought: Naw, nothing queer about him. Got eyes big as platters but he's okay.

Gus got the drinks up and Harland got the

21

whiskey down fast and pushed the glass across the counter for a refill.

Gus said, "Ain't seen you in here before."

"No. I'm from the States."

"Up here on business?"

Harland looked at him.

"Naw," he said, "Something else."

"I'm from the States, myself," Wash put in.

Harland looked at him with a mild expression but Wash had been looked at by plenty of men, in the ring; they looked at you out of the tops of their eyes. Wash was a pretty fair judge of men himself; better than Gus. And the big eyes behind the spectacles didn't distract him; the guy's face was as flat and as hard as an anvil.

"From Detroit," Wash added.

"Have a drink."

Wash hesitated. He hadn't spoken up for that. But Gus poured the drink straight out.

Wash said, "Cheers," lifting the glass.

"Mud in your eye," said Harland.

Take plenty of mud to fill those eyes of yours, mister, thought Gus . . . take a landslide. But he figured he had better not say it.

"I'm in meatpacking, myself," Wash said.

Wash had a horror of being mistaken for a pimp and always got his cards straight on the table when he met a man.

"That so?" Harland said; he said nothing more.

This frustrated Gus, who said, "I'm a bartender."

Harland smiled.

Gus figured he was a pretty cool customer. It took a cool one not to come straight back with his own occupation once another man declared

22

himself. But Gus didn't want to come right out and ask what the guy did, just in case it was something he might be ashamed of. Like he might be a pornographer, say; he might promote feminine hygiene stuff or be on welfare. He might work for the government. It wasn't good to ask.

Then a skinny kid came in with a stack of newspapers under his arm.

"Kid sells papers," Gus said.

The kid moved up behind Wash, shouting about a brutal murder.

"Naw," Wash said, waving the kid away. "Who wants to go reading about a brutal murder?"

Gus said, "That's right. Bad enough some girl gets murdered, without we got to read about it."

The kid scowled, not understanding this at all. He loved to read about brutal murders himself. Too young to frequent bars, he figured these guys were riddled with drink; they must have pickled their imaginations, he thought. He shrugged, shifting the stack of newspapers, and moved back towards the door. Harland James had half turned on his stool, as if to take a paper, but when he saw the newsboy in retreat he turned back to the bar.

"Probably the husband," Wash speculated.

"Eh?" Gus said, eyebrows going up.

"Probably her husband killed her. For cheatin' on him."

"You think so? You hear about it?"

"Naw. But that's most usual the reason they kill em. They catch em cheatin'. They come home, they been workin' hard, they tired, they walk in, what they find? They find some other guy there. He's there, he's pourin' the pork to their old lady, what the hell. They kill the bitch."

23

Gus was clinging to this dusky philosophy, fascinated; James looked amused.

Wash said, "Sometimes they kill the other guy, too. But that don't make no sense. I mean, how you gonna blame the guy? A guy, he gonna get his pussy where he can, right? Ain't his fault, your wife's a tramp; ain't no sense to killin' him. Anyhow, unfaithful wife, she can always find another guy. Husband can't hardly kill 'em all. Husband commences to killin' 'em, he has to stack the bodies up like cordwood. Naw. Take a mean man to do that. So mostly they just kills the wife."

Wash thought about that for a moment, nodding slightly, as if he found the logic sound. Gus was leaning over the counter; he was nodding too. His head went down as Wash's head came up, then it came up as Wash went down, like some reflection out of kilter.

Wash said, "I looked to kill my old lady a few times, bitch as she was. Never did, though. I did, I'd be in jail. So what's the odds?"

"Wife cheated on you, did she?"

"Plenty," Wash said.

He had a twinkle in his eye.

Gus was getting a tremendous thrill from this revelation. He could just picture a sexy black wife cheating left and right; he was imagining all the graphic details of that choice cuckoldry.

"Thing is, she was only a common law wife," Wash said.

Gus didn't want his fantasies diminished.

"It's still cheating," he said.

"And she was a whore," said Wash. "So it wasn't all cut and dried, you see it? Sometimes it was hard to tell when she was cheatin' and when she was workin' . . ."

24

He sighed.

Gus nodded in sympathy and said, "Helluva thing."

And Wash winked at Harland.

Chapter Nine

The newsboy went out into the street, shouting the headlines and waving his newspapers. He was a scrawny youth, tormented by acne and desperate with puberty and he hated selling newspapers; he would rather have been home masturbating. But it wasn't so bad when he had a nice, juicy murder to shout about. He wondered if the girl had been raped before she was killed? Without malice, he hoped so.

Ike Clanton, wheeling down the sidewalk with his great head thrust forward and his mighty arms working like oars, halted beside the boy and held out his hand. The boy gave him a newspaper and held his own hand out for money. Ike, squinting over the headlines, ignored the boy. His eyes darted over the paper, the paper rustled and wrinkled. Then he handed it back.

The boy was dumfounded.

"Hey! You can't read it and not pay for it!" he squawked.

"Get lost," Ike snarled.

"Old cheapskate!"

Ike glowered at him. The boy quickly stepped back out of reach of those powerful arms. He was incandescent with indignation.

"Cheap as you are, I bet you sold your legs!" he shouted.

Ike bellowed and made as if to wheel at him and the boy, terrified, turned and fled. The stack of newspapers billowed like a sail driving him before the wind. Behind him, Ike grinned.

That was pretty good, he thought. Pretty sharp kid. I'll have to remember that line, next time some geezer asks me what happened to my legs.

But then Ike remembered what he'd seen—and heard—the night before and his good humor left him. He had spent a sleepless night. He hadn't minded, either, because if he'd slept he felt pretty sure he would have dreamed about it . . . one of those dreams where you try to run away but you can only move in slow motion and they were even worse for Ike. He shook his massive head. It was none of his business. But still . . . a thing like that . . . he would bet that girl's parents were going to have some dreams themselves. And when they woke up it wouldn't get any better.

Ike was in an agony of indecision.

Going to the police voluntarily was against Ike's principles; offensive to his very nature. Ike refused even to go to the welfare office, let alone to the cops.

But still . . .

Ike felt ashamed of his immobile silence.

In sudden determination, he wheeled off.

Chapter Ten

Wheeling hard, head down and arms churning, Ike almost ran into a postman who, white and shaken, was laboring under his bag. He sidestepped Ike and, the sidestep bringing him to the door of the White Rose, he went in. He stood back from the bar, looking into his bag and pretending he thought there was mail to be delivered there. After awhile he shrugged and sat on a stool. Gus had got the postman's occupation right on the first try and wasn't much interested in him; he was still wondering what the big-eyed fellow did for a living and what Wash McCoy's unfaithful wife looked like. He served the postman a whisky. Then he went back to stand opposite Harland.

"So what brings you to Toronto?" he asked.

Harland had been looking at the telephone on the wall. The damn thing was right there, waiting for him like a time bomb. He had to make that call and he didn't want to and he was glad that the bartender had spoken to him. Uncharacteristically, he felt like talking—but not to Paul, not on the phone, not yet.

He said, "My son lives here."

"Just visiting, huh?"

"Sort of."

Harland had taken his spectacles off and was polishing the lenses. Unmagnified, his eyes were set deep in their sockets and very blue and cold enough to make you shiver. He put the glasses on again. They were like a mask.

He said, "Well, the thing is, Paul is a draft

dodger." He said it as if it was an occupation; he might have said plumber. "He came up here years ago and I haven't seen him since. We . . . didn't agree on things."

"Wife come with you, did she?"

"No. My wife and I didn't agree on things, either."

Wash nodded with understanding.

He said, "That ain't so bad, dodging the draft. Plenty of kids did that, can't be so bad. Cassius Clay dodged the draft and he could fight pretty good."

"Aw, I don't know," Harland said.

He was turning his beer glass around, thumbing the rim as if seeking imperfections in the contours.

Gus said, "They got this amnesty now; kid ought to be able to go home now, he wants to."

"He isn't inclined to. He's not even a kid anymore. The thing is, he met some girl up here . . . here in Toronto . . . and they're living together . . ."

"Ain't married, huh?" Gus said.

Then, aware of Wash, he added, "Not that there's anything wrong with that.

"I thought things were pretty good with him," Harland said. "I hadn't heard from him in quite awhile, last I heard he was okay. Then I got a letter. Well, he sounded pretty damned miserable. So I thought I ought to see if there was anything I could do for him. But hell, maybe he was drunk when he wrote, maybe it amounts to nothing."

The postman glanced up at this talk of letters and drunkeness, as if overhearing heresy.

"Probably found out his girl was cheating," said Wash, getting it into perspective.

Harland grinned. Wash waved at his glass and

28

said, "I'll get this round, I'm earning pretty good."

Harland pushed his empty glass across and said, "I'm going to phone him now." He looked at the phone but made no move. Gus filled his glass. Harland said, "I got here last night and I meant to phone him then but I lost my nerve. Funny thing, being nervous about phoning your own kid. Still . . it's been a long time and we never did agree much on things and . . . and what I mean is, I got to get up and walk over to that phone and call him . . ."

Harland looked sheepish.

He stood up and walked straight back to the telephone, hoping that Paul would answer. He didn't want to talk to the girl. He didn't want to lose his temper and shout, either. But the drinks had helped and he dialed the number.

"Helluva thing," Gus was saying to Wash.

"Helluva thing just happened to me, too," said the postman, as an exordium to ordering another drink. "I'm not supposed to drink on duty, to tell you the truth, but I figure a couple will calm my nerves."

"That so?" Gus said, not interested.

"Yeah. Fact is, I just had a naked girl answer the door."

Gus got interested. He got his elbows on the counter and raised his eyebrows.

"I had this registered letter to deliver, what it was. Pain in the ass they are, too, as a rule. Anyhow, I had to walk up a couple flights of stairs and what with this heavy bag and all I'm sort of winded from the climb. I knock on the door and what happens but this girl opens the door and she's naked."

"Absolutely naked?" Gus asked.

"Couldn't of been more naked. You could see everything."

"Well, I'm damned."

"Could of been anyone at the door, she didn't care. Could of been a bill collector. Could of been a meter reader. Anyone. She didn't care who was there."

"Good looking, was she?" Gus asked.

"Yeah, real cute. Young."

"White?" Wash asked.

"Yeah, white. Not too clean but white. Cute."

'Stacked?" Gus asked, leaning right over the bar now and leering nicely.

"Pretty well stacked, yeah. Nubile, you know?"

"Don't that beat all?" Gus exclaimed.

"Probably lookin' for some postman pecker," Wash chuckled.

"Naw. Had a guy there with her. They got two names on the mail box. Not the same names. What I figure is, I figure they are living together."

The postman downed his second drink.

"Right down the street, it was."

"You don't say!"

"So that's why I'm drinking on duty."

"You can't be blamed for that."

"You wonder why a girl would to a thing like that."

"You surely do," Gus agreed.

Chapter Eleven

Paul James was wondering the same thing, for it was his girl who had answered the door naked.

Her name was Sarah Carlyle and she was still naked. It seemed to Paul that she was naked more often than not, which was fine when they were alone together but not so good at other times. Now she was sitting cross-legged on a large pillow on the floor, a streaky blonde with a good suntan and a trim body. She was opening the registered letter.

She peered into the envelope before she took the letter out.

Paul was standing by the window, looking out and looking angry.

Sarah said, "Daddy sent some more money, Paul."

Paul stared out the window with the long muscles tight down the sides of his jaw. He was flushed. He said, "Money from home," looking out the window and then he turned and looked at the girl. She had glanced up, surprised at his tone. She was a bit haggard at the eyes.

Paul knew that he shouldn't start, shouldn't get her going, but he couldn't help himself. He said, "I just can't figure you out, Sarah. Money from home. How do you justify that?"

Sarah shrugged. She had been known to say "A rich man is as much entitled to his money as a rapist to his victim, no more, no less." Her father was wealthy. Sometimes things were convenient and she didn't say anything.

Paul wasn't really angry about the money,

though. She knew that. She tried to look indifferent and looked insolent.

He got to the point, "Look, I've told you before . . . I don't like you answering the door with nothing on."

Sarah shrugged again. She turned the bank draft over in her hands. "So what?" she mumbled.

"So you did, is what."

"What a bore you can be, Paul."

Paul's mouth opened and he almost shouted at her but he stopped the words in time, so that he was just gaping at her. She laughed.

He said, "Oh, for crissake, honey . . . I mean, sure, it's okay to be a free thinker and believe in women's lib and all that stuff, but hell . . . you got to have some retraints. Or some respect."

"Why?" she asked, playing dumb-innocent and knowing that annoyed him more.

Paul looked around the room.

It was a shabby room. The wallpaper was peeling and there were jagged cracks in the ceiling. The floor was wood and some of the planks were warped. The plumbing was exposed, hot water pipes running across the ceiling and down the wall. Paul figured Sarah liked it that way.

He said, "Society . . ."

"Society is shit," she said.

"But we . . ."

"Society is wrong, it's all wrong. Can't you see that? Sometimes, I think you should have gone to Vietnam and killed a few kids, Paul. Make your father happy."

Paul rolled his eyes. He shrugged. They both shrugged a lot, it was a communication of a sort. He knew he couldn't get across to her and he figured he was getting too old to try now, too old to argue and too old to live in squalor. As he rolled his eyes, the wretched room unreeled in his vision. He walked to the cooler and got a beer.

Then he smiled, without humor.

She had a point, he thought. She didn't know it but she did and sometimes Paul wondered why he had fled the draft. He was no coward, he knew that, and sometimes he wondered if he'd had firm anti-war convictions or had just done the fashionable thing. Those thoughts didn't disturb him much, however. Paul was not given to soul searching. He'd done it, it was done, and now he was living with Sarah because it was the course of least resistance.

He drank some beer, looking out the window again.

The day had brightened and it was getting warmer. People moved in the streets. Sarah was moving behind him but he didn't look; he knew what she looked like. He thought he loved her. He certainly would have married her if she had been agreeable but marriage was not for her. It was out of date and part of the social superstructure that kept the people oppressed. And all the other stuff she spouted. But he did love her, that was the thing. He thought he did. Sometimes he wondered.

He had written to his father the week before, a long, morose, brooding letter. Sarah had gone out and Paul wrote the letter and mailed it before she got back because he hadn't wanted her to see it. Had he waited and read it over later he wouldn't have mailed it, but he did. Now he was a little ashamed of it. It had been too much like soul searching, which he didn't do.

"I'm going to cash this," she said. "Come on, I'll buy you a drink."

Paul nodded.

The phone rang.

Chapter Twelve

Sergeant Joe Greene stood by the library shelves and took the books that the librarian was handing down. They were all books about wolves. Greene had told the librarian he was a cop. He took the books to a long table and began to thumb through them, working on his lunch hour.

Greene was convinced that an animal had killed the girl.

He had seen those thick grey hairs in the wounds and, perhaps more to the point, he was an idealistic young man; he didn't want to believe that a man could do a thing like that. Even a madman was human. He didn't want to believe that a dog would, either. He knew dogs, he had a dog himself. The hairs had been dog-like. Greene would have rather it had been a bear but he didn't figure a bear could be wandering around the city. Someone would have seen it. But a wolf, that was different . . . a wolf could pass as a dog. So now he was reading about them, a passage here and there. From time to time he looked up as he considered something he'd read and he noticed that the librarian was watching him, no doubt wondering why a cop was spending his lunch hour at the library, reading about wolves. But maybe she was only wondering if he was married.

Greene hadn't told LaRoche he was going to the library. If it turned out that a man killed the girl, as LaRoche believed, Greene wouldn't say anything; if his own suspicions were correct, he might be just a little bit smug about his research. Not too smug. He liked LaRoche pretty well. But LaRoche had no imagination, Greene thought. He had a logical mind but was limited by that pattern of thought or way of thinking; he could reason by deduction but failed when induction came into play.

Presently Greene frowned.

All the authorities seemed to argue that wolves were not dangerous to humans and that there were no recorded cases of wolves attacking a human in North America, although there were a few in Russia, where things were different.

Well, maybe he had been wrong, at that.

Still, he had seen that mangled body. How did these experts know, anyhow? Then he had a new idea. He had been reading about the habits of wolves in the wilds and now he wondered if it might not be different with a wolf brought up in a zoo—or even as a pet—used to being around people and without the fear that wild things instinctively feel towards man. Greene figured he had a good idea there. A wolf escaped or turned loose in the city, where there were no rabbits or deer upon which to prey . . . but there were helpless young girls . . .

He tapped his pencil against his teeth, considering.

It would be easy enough to check with all the nearby zoos to see if any wolves had escaped. Or would it? He knew the new Toronto zoo kept the animals in a natural environment and maybe it wouldn't be so simple to take a head count. Still, it had to be possible. They had to know how many wolves they had. On the whole he thought it more likely to have been a pet turned loose but its owner . . . possibly because it had turned vicious and dangerous. That would fit in, all right.

He thought he should take advice on that.

One of the larger books had been published in Canada and Greene turned back to it. There was a paragraph about the author on the back of the dust jacket. N.V. Cronski was an authority on wolves, a founding member of the museum, and lived in Toronto. Greene tapped his teeth with the pencil, then jotted the name down. There was no address but he thought he could check that in the phonebook or through the museum. He thought maybe he would give the man a ring.

He turned to the flyleaf where the man's other works were listed. It was a considerable list and Greene glanced down it to see if anything sounded like a study of wolves in captivity. Nothing did. One entry caught his eye.

Lycanthropy in Fact and Fiction.

What in hell was lycanthropy? It was one of those words that was vaguely familiar, he was sure he had seen it or heard it before but he couldn't think what it meant.

He thought he would look it up in the dictionary.

Then he glanced at his wristwatch and saw that his lunch hour was over. LaRoche would raise hell if he was late getting back today. He forgot about the word for a moment; gathered up the books and took them up to the desk. He thanked the librarian and she smiled at him. Greene noticed that she was quite pretty and wondered if he should mention that he was not married. But he was a bit bashful with girls.

He turned away and then turned back.

"Say, what's lycanthrophy?" he asked.

She blinked and her mouth gave a little twist.

"Lycanthropy is the study of werewolves," she said.

"Oh," said Joe Greene.

Chapter Thirteen

The police pathologist had brought the preliminary report up to LaRoche's office himself, instead of sending it, and they talked for awhile; as soon as he left, Greene came in. LaRoche was staring at the report and he had a strange look on his lean face. Greene waited, curious.

He said, "Well?"

LaRoche looked at him and then his eyes flickered back to the report. Greene moved behind the desk to look over his shoulder and LaRoche sasid, "It's damned strange."

Something in his tone made Greene's scalp prickle.

"They were wolf hairs," LaRoche said.

Greene's eyes narrowed.

He wondered which would have been worse for the girl, in those last terrible moments of her life—a man or an animal? It wasn't a thing you could decide logically. He couldn't figure out which would be worse for himself, let alone the girl. He had leaned over to read the report but LaRoche moved it away.

"I thought so," Greene said. There was nothing smug in his tone. He figured he would mention his trip to the library now, but he wouldn't rub it in. He started to speak but LaRoche snapped the report, cutting him off.

"But . . ." LaRoche paused, staring at the report as if he hadn't understood it and was waiting for the letters to rearrange themselves more comprehensibly. "The saliva in the wounds . . . well, there were two types of saliva. Human and . . lupine."

Greene stared at him.

"Yeah, I know," LaRoche said. "It seems she was bitten by a man and a wolf, both."

Greene said, "I don't get it. How can that be?"

LaRoche fluttered the report back and forth, as if shaking some sense into it. He was thinking.

"I guess I'd better see the inspector on this," he said.

LaRoche stood up and Greene sat down. LaRoche moved towards the door. Before he reached it, it opened and a uniformed cop came in. He spoke to LaRoche. LaRoche nodded. The cop went out and LaRoche came back to the desk. Greene stood up quickly.

"It seems we have a witness," LaRoche said.

He looked hard at Greene.

"Someone saw the *man*," he said.

Chapter Fourteen

"Keep it down, eh?" Paul James said, cupping his hand over the telephone.

Sarah glared at him. She hadn't been making any noise at all and she suddenly had an insight into their relationship—realized that Paul was so accustomed to her shouting about various injustices that he didn't pay enough attention to know when she was shouting and when she wasn't. It reflected poorly on their relationship but she wasn't sure whose fault it was. Sarah had more self-insight than Paul gave her credit for—she just couldn't help herself.

Paul spoke into the phone, waited a moment, then rolled his eyes. Listening to the receiver, he mouthed, "My father," silently to Sarah.

She smiled, drawing her lips back from her teeth.

Paul listened, spoke, listened again. He nodded, as if the gesture could be transmitted over the wires. Sarah watched him. After a few minutes he hung up.

He said, "That was my father."

"So?"

"He's in Toronto. He wants to stop by and see me . . . us . . . this afternoon."

Sarah shrugged.

"Hell, I don't want to have to see him, to explain . . ."

Sarah jumped on it.

"Explain? What's to explain? You did the right thing, you have your own lifestyle, if your father doesn't understand it, the hell with him!"

"Aw, he's my father. I mean . . . I like the guy. It's just that we don't get along."

"So what?" Sarah said.

Paul flared.

"At least he doesn't send me money," he said.

Sarah flushed—or blushed. Paul had struck home. She said, "You want I should rip the bank draft up?" She waved the check at him and then took it in both hands, as if to tear it. Paul didn't give a damn and she didn't tear it. She said, "Hah! Not likely!" She was a bit embarrassed by her aborted gesture, with the bank draft still intact in her hands. "He's my father," she mimicked. "What crap! You were probably just an accident, anyhow. A back seat job!"

Paul blinked. Then he grinned.

"I sure hope so," he said. "I'd hate to be a planned child."

Sarah was startled. After a moment, she grinned.

She said, "Paul, there's hope for you yet."

Chapter Fifteen

The uniformed cop stood back to let Ike Clanton roll on into LaRoche's office. Ike was bristling, furious at having been kept waiting. He rolled right up to the desk. The top of the desk was just at chin level for Ike and LaRoche, staring at him, had the eerie sensation that a disembodied head had been placed before him.

Ike said, "I ain't got all day."

Despite that statement, or maybe because of it, LaRoche said nothing for a few moments. Ike's big head thrust out angrily.

"What can you tell us?" LaRoche asked.

"I told the guy in front. I saw the guy that did the killing. It was just like a movie."

"A movie?"

"A monster movie."

LaRoche got a pen out. Greene was always impressed that LaRoche used a fountain pen. Greene had never owned one. But he didn't notice, now.

"You saw the murder?" LaRoche asked.

"Naw. That was down below. But I saw the killer when he come up from underground."

"What time was this?"

"Aw, I don't know. I ain't got a watch. But I saw him, all right."

"How do you know it was the killer?"

Ike looked astounded. He said, "I saw him. He weren't nothing but a killer. And I heard the girl screaming before that, then this guy comes up. Nothing wrong with my eyes. And this guy . . . like I said . . . like a monster movie." His big torso gave a lurch, a shudder. His platform shifted and his head seemed to float over the desk.

Greene was looking at LaRoche, who kept his face blank.

"You didn't go down when you heard the screams?"

"Of course I didn't go down."

"Why not?"

"Because there ain't no ramp, is why!"

LaRoche blinked. Ike sneered.

LaRoche said, "Why didn't you report this last night?"

41

"Aw . . . I never come to the cops in my life. You know?"

LaRoche knew. He nodded, not angry. He said, "All right. Can you describe him?"

"Course I can. Not much point in comin' here, I can't. First off, I figured it ain't no business of mine. Then I read about it in the paper and got to thinkin'. So I come here. But I been out front, waitin' . . ."

His head turned, gesturing at the door; sliding around with his chin on the top of the desk.

"What did he look like?"

"Big. Sort of big. But in a hunched up way, you know? Maybe not so tall, but big. But his face . . . he's wearing a hat but I got a look in under the brim. There was some moonlight. There was clouds but then the moon come out as he went past me. He was sort of wobbling. Not like he had wooden legs but like he was maybe drunk. Or shook up, on account of what he done. I don't think he saw me. So he looked . . . well, his lips are dragged back from his teeth, see? Like he had a square mouth. And yet. His mouth is dark and wet. I guess that was blood, huh? What the paper said, it was likely blood. A man don't like to see that. a thing like that. See, I'd heard the girl scream, so I figured . . . she screamed on and on . . . seemed like she was screaming for a long time. Suffering. But you can't tell, a thing like that, you can't tell how long . . ."

"All right. What else did you notice?"

"The eyes. When the moonlight hit 'em. It was like the moon had got inside his head and the light was coming out from his eyes like that. Flashin' out."

42

LaRoche was frowning. Greene felt cold.

"What color?"

"Huh?"

"What color were his eyes?"

"Oh, for crissake . . . I don't know."

"What color was his hair?"

Ike looked helpless and irritated.

He said, "Dark. Maybe dark. It was moonlight, I told you it was moonlight . . . everything gets to lookin' black and white in moonlight, don't it? Maybe he had dark hair."

"You'd recognize him again?"

"Oh, yes. Hell, yes."

"We'd like you to look at some pictures."

Ike snorted. "You ain't got no pictures of this guy," he said. "You had pictures of him, you'd know who he was straight off. I mean, it ain't like he was your normal run of the mill Johnny . . ."

"Still, we'd appreciate it if you'd look."

Ike snorted again.

Greene had been trying to speak for some time. Now, avoiding LaRoche's eyes, he said, "But you are sure it was a man?"

"Huh?" Ike said.

"It couldn't have been . . . well . . . a big animal?"

Ike stared at Greene. LaRoche was glaring angrily at Greene, too, but Greene wouldn't look at him.

"Why, I ain't at all sure it was a man," Ike said, surprised, as if that had just occurred to him. "Don't you guys listen? I said, first thing I said when I come in here . . . it was like a monster movie . . ." He wheeled forwards, then backwards; that was the way he fidgeted. He said, "Naw, it wasn't no animal. It was wearing clothes, it's got a hat.

'Course it ain't no animal. But I won't go so far as to say it was a man . . ."

Greene looked at LaRoche then.

Chapter Sixteen

What a shit job, thought Alan Scott of the Kingston Police. He wished he could do it on the telephone so he didn't have to look at the brother but you couldn't do that. You had to go around and tell him face to face. He thought it would be a good idea if the police were issued masks for a job like this. Not masks like bandits wore but masks like they used to wear in old Greek tragedies so that the audience made no mistakes about what emotion you were expressing. You could do things easier when your face was shielded. Scott wondered if he should suggest that to his superiors. He considered. You could have a happy mask for telling some guy that his stolen car had been found undamaged . . . a joyous mask for informing distraught parents that a missing child was unharmed . . . or a tragic mask if the kid had been harmed . . . Maybe even a sadistic mask for making an arrest you didn't really want to make. You could have all sorts of masks. But he guessed they'd think he was crazy if he suggested it. What the hell, they didn't have to do it, why should they give a damn? He had to do it, the task had been delegated to him, and he had only his naked face and he wasn't looking forward to it.

It had fallen to Alan Scott to notify Sandy Dawson's brother.

Her mother was dead and her father was in Vancouver somewhere but she had an older brother in town and how did you tell a girl's brother that she had been murdered? Well, maybe it would have been harder to tell her mother, at that. Or maybe if her mother had been alive the girl wouldn't have gone off to Toronto and got herself killed. There were lots of ways to look at it. But it was a shit job no matter how you saw it. It was your job and you did it and you wished it was over with. Scott quite liked being a cop most of the time. He didn't mind traffic detail, he wouldn't squawk if they transferred him to the vice squad; he didn't mind arresting a guy if he figured the guy was guilty and he postively enjoyed it if the guy gave him any lip. Even the paperwork wasn't so bad. But he wished he had a mask for this one.

He sat behind the wheel of the police car for a few minutes, hoping that maybe the brother would notice the car parked in front and come out to see what it was all about. At least then Scott would be facing him on his own terms, his own territory. But no one came out of the house. Scott sighed. He looked in the rear view mirror, getting his face right. Just solemn enough, just the right touch of sympathy. Not too much, though. What the hell, you couldn't have tears streaming down your face. Christ, he hoped the brother didn't cry! What the fuck would he do if the brother started bawling? Oh, Jesus.

Scott got out of the car and walked up the house step by step.

"Yeah?" said Ron Dawson, looking belligerent

45

and suspicious at the same time. He blocked the doorway, one elbow on the doorjamb, and the other hand on the edge of the door, ready to slam it closed. You just knew he was going to demand a search warrant if you asked to come in.

Scott had taken his hat off.

"Mr. Dawson? Mr. Ronald Dawson?"

"Yeah, yeah. What?"

Dawson had long black hair, carefully greased and swept back into a ducktail. He had a tattoo on his forearm and a couple of jagged teeth. Normally, Scott would not even have spoken to him, except to tell him that he was under arrest. But now he didn't even wince when he called him sir. He said, "I'm afraid I have bad news for you, sir," and it just came out as natural as could be.

"What?" Dawson said. He looked a little worried then.

"May I step in?"

Dawson hesitated. Then he stepped back and opened the door wider. Scott moved into the hallway.

"Well?"

"It's your sister . . ."

Dawson looked blank. Scott figured he was deciding if he should admit to having a sister.

"Sandra Dawson?" Scott said.

"Sandy? What's she done?"

"It's not that, sir."

Dawson was wary, glaring. He wouldn't have been so ugly if he kept his mouth shut, but his lips writhed back in a habitual sneer. He lighted a cigarette. His eyes were on Scott and when he held the match up he missed the tip of the cigarette at first. It went up and down, seeking the flame.

"She's been killed," Scott said.

Strangely enough, that bald statement had no effect on Dawson. His expression didn't change. His hand steadied and he lighted the cigarette and inhaled.

"Naw," he said.

"I'm afraid so, sir."

"Naw."

Scott waited.

"Naw, you made a mistake. Sandy's in Toronto."

"Yes, sir. She was killed in Toronto."

Scott waited. Dawson lowered his hands and left the cigarette in his mouth. He said, "Bullshit."

"She's been identified, sir."

"Naw. What it is, is somebody must of stolen her wallet. With her identification."

"Well, maybe so," Scott said, disliking himself for his weakness. "But they still need you to make the identification . . . one way or the other."

"Where? I got to go to Toronto?"

"Yes, sir. If you will."

Dawson seemed to be thinking about that.

"It ain't her," he said.

Then he said, "Toronto, huh?"

Scott nodded.

"I get my expenses paid?"

Scott had not the faintest idea if the police paid expenses for an identification. He didn't suppose that anyone had ever asked that question before. He said, "Of course, sir." He hoped he would get to arrest Ron Dawson someday . . . not too soon, though, just someday.

"Yeah, okay," Dawson said.

"Do you want someone to drive you?"

"Naw, I got a car."

The bastard don't want to get into a police car, Scott thought. And that was true, but not for the obvious reasons. That would have worried him, riding in a cop car; that would have been like admitting the police were right. Driving himself in his old Pontiac, Dawson just knew it was a mistake.

Someone must have stolen her wallet.

Dawson was furious with his sister.

He'd warned her about the dangers of going to the big city on her own, dammit! Snot-nosed kid wouldn't listen. But a thing like this just showed how dangerous it could be. It wasn't Sandy, no wawy . . . he didn't for a moment worry about that . . . but it could have been Sandy, that was the thing. He hoped it would be a lesson to the girl.

He drove recklessly.

If the police stopped him, he had a fine excuse. He would pretend that he believed the cops were right and nobody would give him a ticket if they thought he was rushing to identify his dead sister. The chumps. He even chuckled about it. But all the way there he didn't even see a cop car and wasn't that just the way life always was. If he hadn't had an excuse, they'd have stopped him for speeding sure as hell . . . .

Sometimes he looked at the bodies.

His name was Tony Hull and he was an attendant at the morgue and sometimes when they brought a dead girl in he got a kick out of pulling her slab out of the wall and pulling the sheet down and looking at her naked body.

He never touched them, though.

48

Sometimes, if they were nubile, he might run his hands along the contours of their bodies, not quite making contact, just caressing their forms as if gently stroking the soul that was rising from the dead flesh. He often got the urge to touch their private parts, but he resisted that unhealthy desire; he figured that would be disgusting, the sort of thing a pervert would do, some nasty necrophiliac. Tony was no pervert. So he just looked and maybe stroked the air above them and got the image fixed real good in his mind so that later, when he masturbated, he had no trouble with the details.

But he didn't want to touch the Dawson girl.

He didn't even want to look at her.

The way she was ripped up, even a pervert wouldn't want to look at her, Tony figured. He was looking at the centerfold of *Playboy* magazine, instead, when Ron Dawson was brought in to make the identification.

Joe Greene was with him.

Dawson stood back from the desk, looking around and wrinkling his nose. He figured the antiseptic smell of the morgue was plenty worse than honest corruption. He felt sorry for the dead girl, whoever she was, being stuck in a place like this.

"Dawson," Greene said, softly.

"Oh, that one!"

Greene glared at Tony but Dawson didn't seem to have heard. Tony left the magazine folded at the center and led them down the corridor. Greene took Dawson by the arm but Dawson didn't seem to need support. He was steady. He looked . . . well, in face, Greene thought, he looked insolent. But that couldn't be. Greene guessed the man was being stoical, holding himself together. It was hard to get into another man's mind, though . . . just as it was hard—impossible, really—to know what thoughts were tumbling around in Sandy Dawson's mind as she died.

When Tony pulled the sheet down, Dawson didn't look. He was running a comb through his hair.

Greene cleared his throat.

Dawson turned and looked at the dead girl.

"Naw, that ain't her," he said and he turned away.

Then he turned back.

His eyes came bulging out and Tony, who was greatly interested in the reactions of the bereaved, almost laughed. They came out just like two hard boiled eggs, he thought.

"Why . . . it is her," Dawson said.

He looked at Greene.

"I warned her," he said.

"Yes, sir."

"She wouldn't listen to me."

"We can leave now."

"Yes, but . . . it is her . . ." said Dawson.

Greene shot Tony a glance and Tony slid the slab back into the wall. Greene took Dawson by the arm again. Dawson was stiff now. His backbone seemed to be moored in the floor, transfixing him, while his flesh melted around it.

"Aw, shit," he said.

In the street, Dawson started to walk away. Greene hesitated. Then he moved after him and offered him a cup of coffee. Dawson shook his head.

"Will you be . . . all right?" Greene asked.

Dawson nodded.

He said, "We weren't close. We were close,

50

maybe she'd of listened to me."

Then he walked off again and Greene let him go.

There was a newspaper kiosk on the corner.

Dawson walked on past it, then turned back and bought a newspaper. It was on the front page. That was good. He didn't have to look for it. He stood there in front of the stand, reading about the murder. He was blocking the front of the counter and other customers were squeezing in around him but the man in the kiosk didn't say anything. He was wondering why Dawson looked so strange. Maybe he got his kicks out of reading about a thing like that; Christ, maybe he was the one that killed her! Lots of madmen liked to read their publicity. It gave the news agent a creepy feeling.

A lot of the details were there.

It seemed worse, somehow, in black and white. It seemed more real. The body would turn to dust in time but the newspaper would be filed away forever and it made the whole thing seem eternal and irrevocable.

Aw, jeez, Dawson thought. They hadn't ought to print stuff like this.

It made him feel dirty.

Chapter Seventeen

"He took it pretty good," Greene said to LaRoche.

LaRoche nodded. He was looking at the

newspaper—the same paper Ron Dawson had bought—and there were other papers spread out across the top of his desk. His face was taut.

"That creep at the morgue," Greene said. "He pulled the sheet all the way down. He didn't have to do that, Steve. He's looking at Dawson and he pulls the sheet right down so Dawson can see . . . well, he took it pretty good."

Greene lighted a cigarette. It tasted antiseptic.

LaRoche snorted. "How the hell do they get these facts?" he said, looking at the paper.

Greene hadn't seen it yet. He said, "What, did they get it wrong?"

"No, damn it . . . they got it right! Thank Christ they didn't get it all. They didn't get the wolf saliva stuff. That's all we need. But this crap . . . how do they know what the condition of the body was?"

Greene shrugged. "They worm it out somehow."

"Jesus! I despise the press . . . the media . . . Why should they go and print details like this?"

"Well, the public has the right to know," said Greene, and the instant he said it he regretted the platitude.

"The public? The public?" LaRoche looked at Greene as if he were demented. "The public has the right to buy newspapers; that's all the right they have. You think they have the right to know about a thing like this? Would you want to know the details if it wasn't your job? I don't want to know how mutilated a body is, if I'm not on the case. Aren't we the public?" Greene had seldom seen LaRoche so agitated. "You think the publishers give a damn about spreading the truth? They want to sell papers, that's all. They squawk about freedom of the press . . . and wallow like playful porpoises in the shit. And the public, the dumb fucking public gets a kick out of reading this stuff. Newspapers created terrorists and sky jackers, right? You know that. They need the publicity. And this killer . . ."

"If he can read," Greene said.

LaRoche looked sharply at him.

"If he's human . . ."

"Don't start that," LaRoche snarled.

He folded the newspaper open—then snapped it shut fast, as if it were some Pandora's box from which the evils of the printed word might leap.

"I knew a guy, once," he said.

He paused. Greene waited. LaRoche peered at Greene as if his face were a cue card on which LaRoche could find the words he wanted to say. But all he found on Greene's face was a look of surprise.

"I knew a guy, once," he said. "In Quebec. He had a big first aid box in his car. Great big fucker. Had everything but an operating table in there. He used to drive up and down the highway all day. Know why? He was looking for accidents. All day, back and forth, eyes peeled for accidents. He'd find 'em, too. Nice, gory accident, he'd slam on the brakes and jump out and administer first aid. That's his excuse for stopping, for being there. He's a good Samaritan. He sees all that blood. He gets blood all over his hands. Maybe he has to administer the kiss of life . . . he gets blood on his face, in his mouth. He sees an arm that's been chopped off . . . just an arm lying beside the road . . . he sees that, he comes in his pants. But he figures he's a good Samaritan . . ."

LaRoche shook his head.

"Reporters are just like that," he said.

Then he said, "This guy . . ." but his references had shifted again. He pointed at the headlines. "This guy, Joe . . . this guy will kill again . . ."

Chapter Eighteen

Linda Drummond was in a foul humour.

She sat on the wharf at Ontario Place, one bare foot hanging down to the water, smoking a cigarette with sullen concentration. She was sixteen years old and had just had a fight with her boyfriend. He'd been looking at other girls all day, the pig, and when she'd snapped at him he'd just walked off and left her and she had no money and, although she walked around looking available, no other boys had approached her. She decided that she hated Ontario Place, anyhow. It was a real drag. She hated Jimmy, too, pig that he was. She figured she might as well go on home, hoping he'd phone so that she could hang up on him. She would, too. She'd slam the phone right down on him. But she had no carfare and would have to walk and that was a real drag, especially since she was barefoot.

A shadow fell across her and she looked up.

A man was looking at her.

But he was old, at least fifty, she thought, so she looked away again and he walked on.

Linda sighed and got up and walked across the

bridge, her pert bottom wriggling in her ripped off jeans. She decided to take a shortcut past the baseball stadium. It wouldn't be much shorter but at least she could walk on the grass. Trudging on, she thought evil thoughts about Jimmy the pig. She was going to get even with him, all right. Just wait until the next time he asked her for a handjob. She wouldn't even touch the damn thing. Or maybe she'd touch it a little, until he got real hot and bothered, then stop. That would fix him. She was eager for her revenge; maybe she wouldn't hang up at that.

She stopped to look in the tavern by the stadium gates but there was no afternoon game and the tavern was devoid of boys. She moved on, forgetting to wiggle her hips.

The stadium was in the Exhibition grounds and she walked past deserted Sno Cone booths and candy floss stands, going around the roller coaster and down a gravel path lined with colorful wagons and caravans. The place was deserted and forlorn, the trappings of amusement sad without people. It made her feel worse because Jimmy had taken her to the Exhibition the year before.

She stopped and opened her cigarette box.

There were only two left.

Jimmy the pig had been smoking her cigarettes all afternoon, damn him. She stood, shifting from foot to foot, trying to decide if she should smoke one now or save both for later. It was a difficult decision for the girl, much the same as trying to decide if she should keep her virginity for marriage.

Then she saw the man coming down the line of wagons behind her, the same way she had come.

It was the same man who had looked at her on the pier, she thought, although she couldn't be sure. He was just as old, anyhow. She wasn't interested. The last thing she was going to do was to give a handjob to an old man.

Still, maybe she could scrounge a cigarette off him.

Old guys usually had cigarettes and didn't mind giving one to a girl. She wondered if she should look young and innocent or young and sexy. If she looked innocent, he might figure she was too young to smoke. But if she looked sexy, he might expect a handjob in return for a smoke. Linda really did have trouble making decisions.

The man was coming.

He had a weird sort of walk, she thought. He almost seemed to be bouncing off the wagons, the way he was lurching. She giggled, thinking that he probably had a big hard on and that it was throwing him off balance. She often had amusing thoughts like that. But she only had two cigarettes and she put her own depleted box away and looked up, starting to smile.

Her smile froze when she saw his face.

Her jaw dropped open.

His jaw was open, too.

Linda was too terrified to run.

She said, "Oh my God," and she just stood there beside the cheerfully colored wagon as he came up to her, staring into that terrible face with her backbone like a spire of ice transfixing her soft, quivering flesh . . . .

Chapter Nineteen

Paul James liked his father, even admired him in some ways. Harland had brought him up after his mother had run off and had tried to be a good father; if they hadn't agreed on many things, well, that was the way things ofen were. Paul was willing to accept at least half of the blame. He guessed that his mother hadn't agreed on many things with his father, either, the way she had finally just left. She'd been a good mother, too, and it was strange how she'd just disappeared with never so much as a postcard to let them know she was all right. The disagreements must have run pretty deep for her to break it off that way, too serious to even discuss. Maybe it was something else. Maybe she had another guy, Paul speculated. He felt sorry for his father when he thought about that. He didn't take sides in it but he felt sorry about it and admired the stoical way that Harland stood up under the circumstances with never a bad word about his runaway wife—a haunted look in his eyes but never a word.

Now he had the haunted look again and the conversation was difficult and strained.

They didn't know what to say to each other.

They never had and the separation of the years had done nothing to bring them closer together now. Paul was embarrassed about the letter he'd sent, the letter that had brought his father here, obviously wanting to help and not knowing how. And Harland was embarrassed at being there, too; he was nervous and uncomfortable. They hadn't mentioned the letter. But Sarah was there and how could Harland bring that subject up in front of her? Paul was dreading being alone with his father. He knew he was going to blush if Harland said a word about that dumb letter. It made him feel annoyed with Sarah, too; if she hadn't been such a bitch he wouldn't have felt he had to mail the letter before she got home and if he hadn't posted it straight off, if he'd considered it and reread it, he never would have mailed it. And that was his fault, too, because he was a damned fool about it; why shouldn't he write to his father? Why should he feel he had to hide that fact from Sarah? Hell, she got checks from her father. Paul didn't fear her scorn or mockery, it was just . . . well, it was just so much easier to follow that course of least resistance. They fought often, and for the most ridiculous of reasons; there was no sense adding more fuel to the fire.

Paul said, "Gee, you haven't changed at all, Dad," and Harland said, "Well, you've certainly grown up, Paul," and they both repeated those stupidities several times. They talked about Toronto; that had changed a great deal and they got some nice neutral conversation out of that. The buildings had changed and the laws had become more liberal. Harland made some joke about how the population of Canada was all huddled at the border, as if for warmth; Paul grinned and Sarah sniffed. They said nothing about draft dodging nor amnesty. They mentioned the gas shortage.

The seconds unreeled with agonizing slowness; time was relative and sluggish.

They had a beer and Paul drank his fast because going to the cooler for another one was something

58

to do. Harland sat with his hands together between his knees and looked around, because that was something to do, as well—but, looking, he saw the peeling wallpaper and the bare plumbing and it only served to make them both less comfortable, although Sarah relished a sense of negative house pride.

She wasn't helping.

She was in a surly, pouting mood because Paul had made her put her clothing on. She thought it would have been delightfully liberated to meet his father naked. She wasn't saying anything and she looked at Harland as if she expected him to say stupid things or suddenly, perhaps, begin cavorting about like a demented clown.

Harland smiled foolishly at her.

He could see why Paul had been taken with the girl. He was no womanizer, himself, but he could see that she was a sexy bit. Not too wholesome, but sexy.

He'd been there for an hour.

"Well," he said.

He looked at his watch and Paul, with relief, figured he was going to make some excuse to leave.

But then he said, "I thought I'd stay a few days, since I'm here. Sort of a holiday. Maybe I can give you dinner or something? I won't want to take up a lot of your time . . ."

"Oh, sure. I'm glad to see you, really."

"Or . . ." He seemed to be desperately searching for something non-committal. "Say, I drove in past the baseball stadium . . . I was wondering . . is there a game maybe tomorrow?"

"I don't know," Paul said.

"Oh. Well, come to think of it, there is. I

59

remember now, I read about it in the paper. The Red Sox will be in town tomorrow. Ahhh. How about if I take you two to the game?"

"Sure," Paul said. He thought that was a good idea; they could spend time together without having to force a coversation; without having to sit there under the bare water pipes with the plaster cracking and the paper peeling all around them. "Sure thing, Dad."

"I hear the Blue Jays are pretty good . . . for an expansion team, I mean. I guess you've probably been following them, huh? I know you used to be a Yankee fan but, living here . . ."

"Well . . . not really." Paul had played baseball in high school. He liked the game. But he didn't follow it now.

Paul looked at Sarah, pleading silently.

Sarah hated that pleading look.

She said, "You won't get me to any damned baseball game."

"Oh. Well . . ." Harland said.

"Aw, honey . . . it might . . ." Paul started.

"I guess you figure it's a boring game, huh?" Harland said. That wouldn't be so bad; anyone was entitled to think a game was boring if they wanted to. But it wasn't that.

Sarah turned her gaze from Paul to his father. She looked spiteful and vicious—far more than she felt. Sometimes she simply couldn't help herself.

She said, "Baseball is a tool of the establishment. Just like the Roman Circus. Games keep the masses entertained so they won't notice what the politicians are stealing . . . and the soldiers are killing."

"Oh, I didn't know that," Harland said, looking as mild and interested as could be.

Sarah blinked. Is he having me on? she wondered. It angered her. He looked dumb with those Coke bottle eyeglasses but just maybe he was being tolerantly amused.

She said, "Well, now you know!"

Paul was rolling his eyes towards the ceiling.

"Ummm . . . still, it seems to me . . . well, all those Christians getting gobbled up by lions and such . . . that does seem a little harsher than a baseball game . . ."

"Well, it's not!" she snapped. And then, because it obviously was, she blushed. Blushing was anathema to a girl like Sarah; she blushed deeper in mortification for blushing to begin with, the vicious circle flushing her face scarlet.

Through her teeth, she said, "No, thank you. But you just run along with Daddy, like a good little boy, Paul."

Now Paul blushed. He was ashamed of her and he was ashamed of himself. He was angry.

Harland wasn't troubled.

He said, "Well, I don't want to be a nuisance. I sure didn't mean to make anyone mad . . ."

He didn't sound slighted. He wasn't perturbed. Paul felt quite proud of his father.

He said, "I'd love to go to the game, Dad."

Harland stood up.

"Well, maybe it wasn't such a good idea . . ."

"No, seriously. I've missed baseball, Dad . . . things like baseball. Sometimes you forget. Let's go to the game."

Harland was nodding, his face blank. His thick glasses flashed as if they were photographing the scene; negatives developed inside his skull. His head turned.

"Okay?" Paul said.

Harland didn't know if Paul had addressed that to Sarah or to him. Neither did Sarah. Paul didn't know, himself.

Harland said, "Well, sure, Paul . . ."

And Sarah said, "Sure, go ahead; I don't mind."

All her anger had ebbed away. She actually smiled without malice.

She was already regretting her refusal to join them. It would have been something different and Sarah was often bored. It might have been fun to watch a baseball game and eat a hot dog.

But to that she could never admit.

Chapter Twenty

Greene had it wrong about LaRoche.

LaRoche was not a man devoid of imagination, not at all. He just kept his head as hard and as tight as he kept his body. He felt as if he could tense and flex the muscles of his mind. Now, while Ike Clanton looked, without enthusiasm, at mug shots, LaRoche was thinking in an orderly fashion about the evidence.

There was no way he would believe that a wolf

had killed the girl—not on its own—but there had to be some way to explain the wolf hairs and the saliva and LaRoche was thinking about a man with a pet wolf. But he didn't like the idea. It fit the evidence but it didn't fit the animal. A dog, yes; a Doberman or Alsation trained to attack, now that was a vicious beast. But the hairs and saliva were lupine, not canine, and LaRoche had to consider the possibility.

Although Greene didn't know it and would have been amazed if he had, LaRoche knew a great deal about wolves. He had grown up in an isolated cabin in northern Quebec where wolves howled through the long white nights and the sound could chill a man to the very bone. But the wolves were not dangerous to man. LaRoche's father had been a trapper and sometimes a wolf would take a pelt from his line but that was all. You could scare them off with a shout or a thrown stick. In captivity, they were more docile than dogs and, although they would always run away given the chance—for the call of the wild was dominant—they would never attack a man. Still, the evidence was there. He had questioned the pathologist and there was no mistake; it had not been a dog.

LaRoche was, in fact, thinking much along the same lines as Greene, but where Greene was considering a wolf that had escaped or been turned loose. LaRoche was more inclined to think of a wolf that had been used by a man—and it was not a pleasant thought.

"Anything?" he asked.

Ike's big head came up, squinting. Then it swung from side to side. He had a torso like a stunted redwood growing out of the platform beneath him and his head would not have been out of place on Easter Island.

"Naw," he said.

"One more thing . . ."

Ike waited.

"The *man* that you saw," he said, stressing the word for Greene's benefit, not Ike's. "He didn't happen to have a dog with him . . . or near him?"

"Naw. Not that I saw."

LaRoche nodded. That meant little; intent on the man, Clanton might not have noticed an animal slinking along low to the ground. And he felt sure that it would have been slinking, too; no animal would have come out of that underground concourse walking high.

"Say . . . how long I been here?"

"Give Mr. Clanton some lunch," LaRoche said.

"Well, now," said Ike, pleased. "Think I might get a little wine with it?"

"Certainly," said LaRoche.

He headed back towards his office. Greene followed, thinking about what LaRoche had asked Ike. The everyday, run of the mill work was going on in the station but there was an undercurrent of tension, a vibrancy. This wasn't New York or Chicago—which made the police proud—and murder was not so very common here, especially one as brutal as this. Everyone was a little excited.

The telephone was ringing in his office when LaRoche went in.

It was his wife, asking him to pick up some steaks on his way home. LaRoche was disoriented by this contrast between his job and his home life and he stared at the phone for a few moments before he answered. He noticed that he had a smudge of ink on his thumb. That was a contrast, too; it wasn't blood.

"I may be a little late tonight, Stella," he said. She didn't even hear him.

"There's been a murder," he said.

"Yes, dear . . . but don't forget, the larder is bare," Stella said. She laughed, a light, tinkling sound. Stella never took the slightest interest in his work and never told people what he did, if she could help it. She seemed to think being married to a cop was beneath her, that it was undignified. He had to deal with criminals and sordid crimes and things that had to be done but were not spoken of in polite company. Stella was an elegant, stylish blonde with a tendency towards social climbing. But she was all right. She didn't nag him and—LaRoche was glad to this—didn't seem to worry about the possible dangers of his work.

"If I'm going to be very late . . ." he said.

"If you can stop at Kensington Market, darling . . . you can get by far the best buy there . . ."

" . . . I'll phone and let you know . . ."

"And, perhaps, a bottle of wine?"

LaRoche sighed. "Yes," he said. He was not annoyed; she could have been worse. He put the plhone down and it rang again before his hand had left it.

It was Billings, calling from home.

They spoke for a moment. Then Billings spoke and LaRoche listened and then there was silence while he stared at the wall and frowned.

"Come over here now," he said.

"I'm not on duty until . . ."

"What?" LaRoche said.

"I'm on my way," said Billings.

LaRoche put the phone down again. He kept his hand on it, as if he expected it to ring again . . . or was placing it under restraint. He was thoughtful.

"Steve?" Greene said.

"We may have a second witness," LaRoche told Greene.

Chapter Twenty-One

The first witness had finished the lunch that had been brought in to him. He was lingering over the glass of wine and wondering if he might be on to a good thing here. If he came back tomorrow and offered to look at some more pictures, they would probably give him lunch again. It was worth a try, even thoiugh he knew damned well they didn't have a picture of that guy. But there was no sense in looking at any more pictures now. He was full and there was only the one glass of wine and that was sort of small.

He looked around. They'd left him alone to eat and he wasn't under arrest. He wheeled out of the room and down the long hallway. He passed a few cops but none of them paid any attention to him.

He went out the front door. There was no ramp. He had to get a grip on the railing and go down the steps like a sidewinder.

He'd reached the pavement when aw thin, bald guy in a striped jacket came out and hurried after him.

"Mr. Clanton?" he said.

Ike nodded. Everyone was addressing him with respect today. He didn't mind. It was bullshit, but it was okay.

"I'm Art Rose," the man said. He mentioned a newspaper.

"Reporter, huh?"

The guy squatted down so that he was level with Ike. He had a notebook in his hand. Ike thought he looked like he was taking a shit and had a handful of toilet paper. Ike really hated it when guys squatted down, especially a guy like this that wasn't so tall to begin with. Bald, too. Ike had plenty of hair and when he'd had legs he never squatted down.

"I understand you witnessed this murder last night?"

"Naw."

"Oh? I was under the impression . . ."

"Saw the guy that did it, though."

"Ah . . . perhaps . . . the police are being rather reticent about the whole affair . . . not being helpful at all, in fact. Perhaps you'll grant me an interview?"

"Naw," Ike said.

"No?"

"What I said."

"But, surely . . . It's your duty, sir."

Ike held no brief for duty and he didn't like men who referred to it. It annoyed him.

"If you could just describe him," Rose said.

"Now, what's the point in that?" Ike said.

Rose gaped at him, confused. Everybody liked to get their name in the paper.

Ike said, "I described him to the cops. That's 'cause it falls to them to catch him. You know? You gonna catch him?"

"Why, that's not . . . I mean . . ."

Ike snorted and wheeled away. Then he wheeled right back, his face furious.

He said, "You know that crap about the pen being mightier than the sword? That's crap. Cop in there, he's got a pen. A real one. Fountain pen. He's got a gun, too."

Ike wheeled away again; again he came back.

"You look like an asshole, too," he said.

Then he felt better and he rolled off. Neither of them had understood this exchange at all. Rose didn't know what Ike was saying and Ike didn't know why he said it.

But he felt pretty good about it.

Chapter Twenty-Two

Waiting for Billings to arrive, LaRoche sat at his desk and tapped his fountain pen on the surface and Greene stood at the window with his hands clasped behind his back. The steady tap-tap made him nervous. Somehow it made him think of blood dripping off the dangling fingers of a corpse and falling sluggishly to the floor.

Greene said, "Steve, I don't know exactly how you're thinking about this . . . and I don't want to make you mad . . . but . . . well, shouldn't we check with the zoo?"

The fountain pen tapped once more and stopped.

"I already have," LaRoche said.

"Oh," said Greene. Then: "When, Steve?"

"While you were at lunch."

"Before you got the pathologist's report?"

"That's right."

"Then you did think it was possible that . . ."

The pen tapped sharply, like a full stop to Greene's sentence. LaRoche said, "I thought maybe the zoo keeper did it." Then he shrugged.

Greene had his jacket off, slung over the back of a chair. Now he unbuttoned his cuffs and rolled his shirtsleeves up, two turns to each. He pulled the knot of his necktie down. This easing of his clothing was the counterpart of LaRoche's precise fountain pen tapping. Greene was not as methodical in his thoughts and did not keep his mind channeled; his ideas jumped about.

Greene was pleased that, despite his statements, LaRoche had not excluded the possibility of a wolf.

But now they had a witness.

Greene said, "That guy is creepy, sticking up off that platform. The way he described the man he saw come out from underground . . . it gave me goosebumps, Steve.''

"Not, I think, a reliable witness; possibly drunk at the time. But he saw something. He's not the sort to come to us on a whim. And whatever he saw . . . still . . ." LaRoche seemed to be having trouble deciding what line he was taking . . . "A man who had just killed like that . . . who was capable of killing like that . . . well, he's got to look pretty damned strange afterwards, if not before. You see what I'm getting at?" He looked at Greene. "I mean it's not strange that he looked strange." He paused again; added, "A man who did a thing like that."

"Or saw it done," Greene said.

"What?"

It had been a flash of an idea and Greene took a moment to think it over before he spoke.

He said, "We've been assuming that the man Clanton saw killed the girl. That's not necessarily so. Suppose he just happened to be walking through the underground concourse and saw the girl killed? It's not unlikely that he might have been in shock; wandered off in a daze, looking . . . strange . . ."

LaRoche hadn't thought of that; he castigated himself even as he congratulated Greene on seeing the possibility.

"If that's the case, maybe he'll come forward. . . after the shock wears off."

"Maybe. Lots of reasons why people don't want to come forward, Joe. Even innocent people. Still . . ."

"It is possible, though. Right?"

LaRoche looked at him, wondering what he was getting at.

70

"Which still leaves open the possibility that the killer was not human," Greene added.

"A wolf," said LaRoche.

"Something," said Greene.

Billings arrived shortly.

"Well, naturally," he was saying, "I figured this guy was a fruit cake, didn't pay it much mind. I mean, you don't do you? Some of the things you get. Anyhow, I went right to bed after my shift so I didn't hear about the murder until just now. When I phoned you. It most likely ain't nothing, anyhow. But still . . . it's not far from the King Eddie to Eatons and the time element is about right . . . so I thought you ought to know."

He looked back and forth between LaRoche and Greene. Billings had never been closely involved in a murder case and he hoped the homicide team would be interested.

"Let me get this straight. He said that it was an animal, definitely an animal?"

"Yeah, he was certain of that. It wasn't a man wearing a mask, it was an animal. He didn't know what sort."

"It fits, Steve . . . the eyes glowing and . . ."

"We have another witness," LaRoche told Billings. "Your man may not have been crazy, at that."

"Jeez," Billings said.

It was exciting. It was sort of scary.

"You think maybe it was like the *Murders in the Rue Morgue* or something?"

They looked at him and Billings blushed.

"You know . . . the story where an ape . . ."

"We know," LaRoche said.

"I just thought . . ."

"We're not sure what to think, as yet."

Billings nodded. He wanted to say that the whole thing was sort of spooky, but he figured that homicide teams didn't say things like that.

"We want to keep it sort of quiet, right?"

Billings nodded. He hoped they'd tell him more.

Greene said, "Shall I go see this guy from the King Eddie?"

"I'll be glad to see him," Billings put it. "Even though I'm not on duty, I'll be glad to . . ." He wanted to get involved and he didn't want the guy telling Greene that he'd been sort of sarcastic to him. Especially now that the guy might not be such a nut, after all.

"No, that's all right, Billings," LaRoche said. "Thanks for dropping by . . . on your own time."

Billings saw that LaRoche could get sarcastic himself.

He also saw, with regret, that he was being dismissed. He got up. He hesitated, holding his hat in his hand, as if he didn't know if he should put it on before or after he left the room. He said, "Well, anything else I can do . . ." but LaRoche was moving his fountain pen back and forth and as his wrist tilted down the pen pointed at the door.

Billings left.

LaRoche was silent for a time.

Greene rolled his cuffs up another fold. He was wondering what in hell the man from the King Eddie could have seen? He had a few ideas, none of which he cherished.

LaRoche said, "I don't know."

Greene said, "What's that, Steve?" but LaRoche had been talking to himself.

"I don't know a fucking thing," he said.

72

Nothing he was going to express, at least.
"Go see this fruitcake," said LaRoche.

Chapter Twenty-Three

Well, it could have been worse.

Harl came out of Paul's apartment building and headed down toward the White Rose, thinking that the meeting with his son could have been plenty more difficult. It hadn't been comfortable, but he hadn't expected it to be after so long . . . and Paul had seemed genuinely pleased to see him. The girl was a strange sort, though. Harl guessed she was what was called a hippy. Maybe that term was passé, he wasn't sure; it wasn't a word he favored. At least Paul didn't have long hair, that was something; out of all proportion, it seemed crucial. The Vietnamese boat people would have long hair, he reckoned; they had no food or water, they sure as hell wouldn't have barbers on board as they starved on the boats and wondered who had betrayed them. But he was glad that he hadn't got into that with Paul and Sarah. Even if it was right, it would have been wrong . . . and Harl wasn't even sure he was right. Sometimes he thought he failed to understand things.

He'd had two beers at Paul's; they had tasted metallic and made him thirsty. He'd been drinking more, lately. When he came to the White Rose, he turned in.

Gus was glad to see him. Gus was always glad when a customer returned; it was just like a friend coming to call.

Gus said, "See your kid today?"

Harl nodded and slid onto a stool.

"How'd it go?" Gus asked, a wolfish nosiness cloaked in a sheepskin of a concern.

"Okay, I guess."

Gus held a shot glass up; Harl nodded. Gus poured him a measured shot of rye and pulled a beer. Harl leaned over the bar, on his elbows. He didn't look as if he felt like chatting and this perturbed Gus. But then Wash McCoy came in, weary from work. He groaned as he mounted a stool, then sighed.

"Meat," he said and, as if that was self-explanatory, he said no more. He had a drink.

Suddenly Harl brightened.

He said, "I'm taking Paul to the baseball game tomorrow." That seemed important and interesting. "His girl won't go, though," he added.

"Yeah, but girls don't like baseball," Gus said.

"She said it was like the Roman Circus," Harl said, grinning. "Said it kept the masses happy."

"She say that? What kind of shit is that?"

Wash chuckled in his throat. "Kids," he said.

He looked into his glass as if it were a crystal ball.

"These youngsters . . . the way I see it, they got no focal point. These kids. Our generation, we knew what we had to do. We knew what we were.

74

A pimp, he had to pimp. Burglar had to burgle. Cop, he had to cop . . . had to arrest the burglar if he could. They're both doing their jobs, no hard feelings. But this new generation, they don't know what they are or what they got to do. They ain't got it in focus. You take your dyke, now. In our day, a dyke was a dyke, right? Nowadays, they is all bisexual. They don't know what they are. What kind of crap is that, a gal don't know if she likes boys or girls?''

Gus was wondering if Wash's unfaithful wife might have been one of those things?

"But they know they got to do something," Wash said. "They sense it. Like animals. Animals got these instincts. They know they got to migrate or build a nest or fertilize some eggs. They got vague compulsions to do these things; they don't maybe know why they do 'em, but they do. It's the same with these kids. They got to carry a banner or vandalize a graveyard just to be doing something. That's how I see it."

Harl was listening attentively, as if he attached great importance to these words. Gus, who did not quite understand it, had his mouth open. And Ike Glanton rolled in on his platform in time to hear the conclusion of the philosophical statement.

Ike had done a bit of desultory panhandling on his return from Jarvis Street and he had money for a drink.

"That hold true for killers, too?" he asked.

"Killers?" Wash said.

"Gimme a shot, Gus," Ike said. He was scowling. He wanted to tell them that he had been a witness. It wasn't like having it in the newspapers, these were his friends. But he didn't want them to think he was boasting. And he hadn't done anything, either; he had just been there and he'd kept still and quiet.

"You got money?"

Ike slammed some change on the bar.

"Yeah, killers. Like this murder last night."

"Why, I wouldn't know about that," Wash said. "I heard there was a murder, is all."

"Wash figures it was an irate husband," Gus said.

Ike nibbled around the edges of it then said, "Naw, it weren't no husband."

"How you know?" Gus asked.

"Saw the guy," Ike said, off-handedly.

"Naw!"

"Yeah. Saw him come up from underground."

"You never did."

Ike looked around, his wheels scraping sideways on the floor. He looked at Harland James, who was a stranger, challengingly.

"Is that a fact?" Harl said.

"Yeah. Nothing to be proud of. Just happens I saw him. I been in the police station all afternoon, come to that; looking at pictures of suspects and such."

"Well, I'm damned," said Gus.

"But how you know it wasn't a husband?" Wash asked.

"That fella was never nobody's husband, tell you that. Way he looked, no one would of married him."

"That so? What'd he look like?" Wash asked.

But Ike didn't want to get into that. That was pretty far-fetched and he might as well keep to the edge of belief.

76

He shrugged.

"White, was he?" Wash asked.

"Yeah. Sort of."

Wash looked puzzled. Ike lowered his chin and looked sullen. His indecision had made him surly. He refused to say anything more about it.

By the time Harland James left the White Rose the sky was dark and the moon was out . . . .

Chapter Twenty-Four

The moon was full and it was striking down on Joe Greene's profile through the car window. Greene was at a drive in movie with Bonny Cutter, a girl he sometimes dated. Timid with girls, he liked to date Bonny because her boldness complemented his shyness. Often she took the initiative.

Greene had almost forgot about his date.

He had gone to the King Edward to interview the witness, fruitcake or not, but the guy wasn't in his room. He was still registered but he was out. Greene had left a message and walked out past the bar. He had taken Bonny there for a drink once and he remembered he'd ask her to go to the movies. Now he didn't feel like it but he didn't feel like much of anything, really. It had been a long day. He'd phoned her to verify the date and Bonny was expecting him to pick her up and so now he was sitting in a drive-in theater, thinking about the murder, with Bonnie snuggling up to him.

They were watching *Superman*.

It was shit, Greene thought. He liked things that were real.

Bonny was real enough, cuddling up against him affectionately. But Greene was distracted.

"You're in a funny mood, Joe," she said.

"Sorry. It's this damned murder . . . or whatever."

"Whatever?"

"Well . . ." he hesitated. LaRoche would have skinned him alive if he knew it, but Greene said, "Well, there's some doubt that a human killed a girl . . . it might be an animal."

Bonny stared at him.

"My goodness! Surely you know."

"Yeah . . . but it wasn't a normal sort of crime." Already he regretted saying anything about it.

"The papers said it was probably a madman."

"I guess it was."

"Said she was all clawed and chewed," Bonnie went on. She did not seem at all disturbed by the idea.

"Yeah, some maniac," he said.

Bonny giggled.

"Nymphos are maniacs, too," she said.

Greene looked at her. It didn't register.

"Nymphomaniacs? You know?" she said.

"Aw, jeez . . ." he said.

Bonny was miffed. She drew back to her own side of the seat and lighted a cigarette.

"I guess I'm not such good company, tonight," he said.

"You sure aren't."

"If you'd seen that poor girl . . ."

"All chewed, huh?"

He nodded with the moonlight running down his face.

"I just can't understand how a man could do a thing like that," he said. "I mean, a rapist . . . well, I'm not about to rape a girl, but I can sort of understand why a guy would. I guess I can understand it. A sex fiend . . . well that's human, is what I mean. But this . . ."

"Was she raped?"

Greene shook his head. "No," he said.

"Don't sound like a sex fiend, to me," Bonny said. "What the papers said, sounds more like a cannibal."

Greene stared at her in amazement.

Bonny, miffed and amused at the same time, said, "I wouldn't mind if a cannibal ate me . . . as long as he was good-looking and started at the crotch . . ."

Greene looked so funny when she said that that Bonny began to laugh. She snuggled up to him again. But he sat there like a lump of iron and, to her annoyance, Bonny realized that he was not interested in her body and not charmed by her wit. It was going to be a lousy night, she thought. On top of that, she didn't like the movie, either. She, too, liked real things.

That dead girl had been real.

Greene couldn't stop thinking about it and he wondered if the killer would strike again. He wondered where and when, not knowing what was already under that colorful caravan outside the stadium. . . .

Chapter Twenty-Five

There were clouds that night.

The full moon was washing the whole city with light and the tall buildings stuck up like tombstones under the black vault of the sky. Light poured over the rims of roofs and ran down the sides of houses and spilled like quicksilver into the streets. It pooled a shadow at Harland James' feet as he paused for a moment to light a cigarette outside the White Rose. As he walked on, it folded in a sombre blanket around his feet and clung tenaciously to his stride. Slightly drunk and thoughtful, he didn't notice.

But Billings noticed it as he walked to the precinct, on night duty again. It was just about the brightest moonlight he'd ever seen, he thought; a man could trip over those shadows, solid as they were; he could stub his toe on those moonbeams. But then, there were plenty of things over which a man could stumble. You had to watch your step.

Billings was unhappy.

When he'd come out of LaRoche's office earlier, Art Rose had pounced on him. Rose assumed that Billings was working on the murder and Billings, who wished he was, did not disabuse the reporters. But it had been frustrating as hell because there was nothing that Billings could reveal. He would have liked to have his name mentioned in the paper as the alert officer, due for promotion, who had made a vital discovery. Pride came with publicity, and success and, after all, it was only fair . . . he had made the connection that lots of men would have overlooked. But LaRoche had told him to keep it quiet and, dutifully, he'd told Rose nothing. It had frustrated both men. Rose instinctively knew that certain facts were being kept from him and he seethed with indignation, but it was worse for Billings, who was doubly confounded. It wouldn't have been so bad if he were actually working on the case and could follow up on the lead he was unable to mention. He might even had been smug about his silence, in that case. But as it was he got neither credit nor satisfaction. LaRoche got his name in the papers, you could bank on that, and Billings had been sorely tempted to talk to Rose. Yet there was another dilemma: if Rose used his name, he would get hell for it, it not censure; if he was merely quoted as an unnamed source, he got no glory. Either way, you lose, he thought; you might as well hit your head against the wall; you might as well bounce it off a moonbeam.

He stepped cautiously through the shadows.

Jessie Drummond stood at the window, looking out.

Flooded with moonlight, the window was an opaque silver shell. Brilliantly lighted, it illuminated nothing. But Jessie was looking out, anyway. He was a rangy man, wearing an undershirt and baggy trousers and carpet slippers. He had a long jaw and along that jaw the muscles were tight. He was slowly driving his fist into the open palm of his hand as regularly as if he were punctuating the passage of time by a manual metronome.

"Where in hell is she?" he said.

He had said that frequently.

Behind him, his wife fluttered about the room, furiously dusting the furniture. Where her husband's movements were steady, hers were erratic; she, too, was marking the moments as she moved.

"Where in hell is she?"

"Hadn't we better call the police?"

"Where in hell . . ."

"I think we should call the police."

'What the hell for?"

"It's late, Jesse."

"I know it's late."

"Well, then . . ."

"What if she's shacked up with some guy? Huh? You want to call the police, they find her shacked up with some guy?"

"She isn't with Jimmy. I phoned."

"I know you phoned, for crisssake. I was here when you phoned. He ain't the only guy around, is he? I'll break his fucking neck, she's with him. What if she's there with him while he's talking to you on the phone? You think of that? What's he gonna say? They're in bed together, they got no clothes on, he gonna tell you that? What are you, dumb?"

"Maybe . . . Jesse, maybe it's something else . . ."

She was nervous; afraid to say it. She knew her husband was given to terrible and misdirected rages.

He turned and squinted at her. The moonlight flowed around behind his head. He looked like some fierce trophy mounted on a silver plaque.

"What else?"

82

"I . . . don't know."

"She's with a guy. I'll break her neck."

She sat down. She was still holding the feather duster and she moved it back and forth like a fan. His eyes shifted with it. He said, "She takes after you. She's a tramp."

"She's never stayed out before."

"Why in hell did you let her go out?"

His wife looked at him, bewildered and frightened.

"Jesse . . . honey . . . she only went to Ontario Place with Jimmy. What do you want me to do? Keep her locked up in her room all day? She's sixteen . . ."

"She's a tramp."

His face was dark with fury.

Knowing his anger was misdirected and unreasonable, Jesse felt guilty; feeling guilty himself, he became enraged with his wife.

"You dumb bitch," he said.

They waited for Linda to come home.

She was going to catch hell for this . . . .

They'd had wine with dinner and, a bit tipsy, Sarah Carlyle felt romantic. She looked out the window and thought that the city was beautiful in the moonlight. It looked like an ivory miniature from which an ebony lid had been lifted. It looked like some idyllic future world, where injustice had been banished and oppression lifted and spotless slums were preserved as a reminder of the past. But Sarah was Sarah. She sighed. She could still see the shadows.

Paul could see her, silhouetted at the window.

She was naked and her outline looked as if she were wearing jodhpurs, with her slim torso and sweeping hips. He felt a surge of desire as he waited for her to come to bed—to the mattress on the floor, actually; they had no bed. He knew her moods and knew she would be agreeable to sex this evening. They had gone to dinner at a Greek restaurant and drank resinated wine and Sarah had got affectionate, as she always did in ethnic surroundings. Having never been out of Canada, she adored all things foreign. It had not gone so well at first. After his father had left, there had been a tense silence; they both anticipated an argument. When no argument arose, they were both surprised and pleased. She had yawned a few times, faking it deliberately, but that was the worst of it. And then—with her money from home—she decided they should go out to a restaurant and it had been a great success.

"I wish it was like that now," she said.

"Hmmm?"

"The world . . . like ancient Athens."

"There was Sparta," he said.

"You bastard."

"They had slaves. They called them Helots."

"Oh, don't!"

"Hemlock . . . they had hemlock, honey."

She turned at the window. He could not make out her countenance but he knew she was not angry; he could tell by the way she moved, pneumatic and supple.

"Socrates . . . he kept slaves . . ."

"He never did!"

Paul hadn't the faintest idea if he had or not but he said, "He certainly did."

"Oh, don't ruin it . . ."

"And buggery . . . plenty of buggery . . ."

"That's not so bad."

"Come to bed."

She moved towards him. In the dark room, her body seemed to cast a soft golden light; she glowed in the dark. She came slowly to the mattress, knowing that Paul was watching her. Sometimes when he teased her she flared up angrily; at other times she seemed as naive and innocent as a child. Paul knew there was no point in speculating which way she would react at any given time; it had no pattern; she was random and unpredictable and when he was of a mind to tease her, he did so without hesitation. It was all right this time. She stood over him, incandescent and vibrant, soft and pliable; she trembled with passion exactly as she trembled with anger and she was trembling now. She came down as if she were unwinding into his arms.

She hovered over him.

The mattress was lumpy under him and she was smooth and moist above him and if she chose the dominant position it was a small concession to her equality, a welcome manifestation of her liberation. Soon she began to whimper.

It could always be like this, he thought; if only it were always like this . . . .

Like silver-backed fish, cars moved along the highway, their headlights insignificant in the bright moonlight. But the moon did not light everything. It could not seep under things. The cars dragged shadows beneath them as they glided past the empty stadium; the stadium was ghostly with elongated slats of darkness under the seats and the Ferris wheel laid an intricate filigree on the ground, a round net of shadows.

The oblong tops of the wagons and caravans were illuminated and beneath them the gloom was deep and there were dead things in the dark . . . .

Chapter Twenty-Six

I seem to have pinned myself to Toronto like a moth to a collector's board, Paul had written. Since he was drunk and morose, it had seemed a clever simile; he'd thought it would impress his father. He had written other things. In fact, Paul didn't quite remember just what he had said in that regrettable, whining letter but he knew they were embarrassing in style and content. Harl James had kept the letter.

He read it again, as he waited for room service to bring his breakfast.

Harl had a slight hangover courtesy of the White Rose, but it didn't bother him. If your head ached and your bones were a little stiff, what the hell . . . you knew you were alive.

The letter bothered him, though.

Paul had seemed happy enough the day before. A bit tense and uncomfortable, sure, but that was natural. The girl, though . . . well, she could have been worse.

He folded the letter and put it away.

He moved to the window and gazed out. It was a glorious day, a great day for a ball game.

Harl phoned Paul.

"Dad's going to pick me up outside," Paul said.

He glanced at Sarah.

"So he won't have to find a parking space," he added.

"Or see me again?" she said.

Paul said, "Oh shit."

The night before she had been warm and soft and pliable; now she was cold and hard and rigid. He could almost see the facets in her face reflecting her mood like points of light in a diamond. But he could not define that mood. Sharp as it was, it was blurred at the edges. She was not naked. She had actually put clothing on as soon as she got up and it was no concession to Paul; she was donning armor. Paul started to speak several times. His mouth would open and no words would come out and he would close it again before she turned and found him with his jaw hanging open like a beached fish.

He wanted to ask her to go with them.

But he was afraid that such a plea would bring only scorn, maybe outrage. He said nothing. He got dressed. She was banging around the flat, moving things not putting them in order, merely shifting random patterns to new disorder.

Paul put a necktie on.

When he had knotted it, he faced her, waiting for her to mock his conformity but she looked away.

"Well . . . I'd better go down," he said.

"Um hum."

"I'll be back after the game."

"I guess you will," she said. "I might be here."

Paul went downstairs to wait.

Oh damn! Sarah thought, as soon as he had closed the door. She had been hoping desperately that he would ask her to go with them. She wanted to. She was determined to be pleasant to his father and, if she did not enjoy the game—she didn't know, she had never been to a baseball game—she would at least not bitch about it. But because she longed to go, she felt vulnerable and defenseless and so, being Sarah, she put up her shield of cold indifference and defeated her purpose. Paul had not asked. Why should he ask, when she was storming around in a fury? She thought: hoist by my own petard. And then she thought: what the fuck is a petard? She smiled at that. She would have been willing to bet that ninety-nine out of a hundred people didn't know what a petard was. But that did her no good. She was still there alone and she was bored; it was going to be an awful day.

She tried to read a book.

The letters flitted around like random electrons; she could make no sense of them.

She wishes they had a television set.

Paul had wanted to buy one; she had told him that television had replaced religion as the opiate of the masses and he had not insisted. Maybe opiates weren't so bad. She smoked marijuana sometimes; she didn't much like it and she never smoked it when she was alone. In company, she did. She sucked the smoke right in and said, "Oh, wow," and things like that. She said, "This is good shit," sometimes. It made her hungry. She was hungry now. She could have had a hot dog at the stadium. But she probably wasn't really hungry, she was most likely just bored.

She didn't want to go out.

She knew where that would lead. Some guy would try to pick her up. He'd probably have a wheel of hair all around his head and if she spurned him he'd think she was a prude. He might, for crissake, accuse her of virginity. And if she went with him she would have to screw him; she'd have to instigate an oral prelude to the act, as well, so he'd be assured she was sexually liberated. And she didn't even like to do that.

She stayed home.

Her outrage simmered.

The coffee was simmering by the time that Anna Drummond had made up her mind that she was going to call the police. She had a cup first. Jesse had not gone to work. Linda had not come home and Jessie seemed very quiet and calm. He had raged about the night before; in the wee hours he had become quiet, although he had not slept. She knew he was worried about Linda and that he found it hard to express an emotion as tender as concern. She wondered why she had ever married Jesse. Well, she knew why. She had been pregnant, was why. She wondered why she had never divorced him and she knew the answer to that, too. Because of the child. It was a vicious circle. She thought that if anything had happened to Linda, she would go to a lawyer and file for divorce. That was the first thing she would do. She could picture herself marching determinedly into a lawyers office and . . and why was she thinking of a thing like that?

Linda had spent the night with a boy.

Jesse was right . . . he had to be.

He hadn't shaved and he had a heavy, dark beard. He was a ferocious looking man. He beat her frequently. Now Anna walked up to him and she put her hand in his face. She got a good grip on his bristly cheek and twisted, so that his flesh rolled up and his head tilted.

"I'm phoning the police," she said.

Jesse nodded. He was mild as a lamb and his cheek twisted in her fist as he nodded.

"Should've . . . last night," he said. Then he said, "I will."

And he did.

He only had to talk for a minute. The police said they would send someone around immediately. When he hung up, Jesse looked amazed. He rubbed his cheek, where his wife had brutalized his flesh and he looked absolutely amazed that such a timid woman had done that to him . . . and that the police had shown such consideration and efficiency. The cop on the phone had even sounded . . . worried. That was strange . . . it wasn't as if it was the cop's daughter who was shacked up with some guy . . . .

Chapter Twenty-Seven

"How can you live in a city that don't sell beer at a baseball game?" Harland asked, but he was smiling when he said it and Paul smiled back. It was a valid point, he thought; he had often remarked on the strange blend of sophistication and naivity that made up this city. Despite welcoming draft dodgers from the States, the Canadians were fiercely patriotic themselves. They thought they'd won the War of 1812 and refused to believe that the English had been involved. They believed that Alexander Graham Bell was a Canadian; they'd built a tower, the only function of which seemed to be interference with television reception and maintained that the Pontiac was a Canadian car. And beer was banned at their big league park.

"Sorry, Dad," Paul said.

Paul was feeling good.

It was a good thing to be at a baseball game with your father, he thought. It was proper. They were talking more easily now, in the open air, without the crumbling plaster—and without Sarah to confound them. It was nice to be away from Sarah for awhile, he had to admit it. He loved her but she was just too much, sometimes she was just too much.

Harl was signaling a vendor.

"Want a hot dog?" he asked.

"I sure do," said Paul, with true enthusiasm.

Sarah was not there to ruin that. She could ruin anything, Sarah. She could spoil heaven.

Paul grinned at the thought, chomping away on

the hot dog and grinning hugely. He was thinking of Sarah in paradise. It was a dandy thought. When Sarah died and went to heaven she would waste no time before she started organizing protest marches demanding equal rights for fallen angels. He could just see it. There was strident Sarah storming through the fleecy clouds, her halo slightly askew, defiantly holding up her banner as she led a band of obedient saints and disgruntled cherubs in picket before a bemused God.

Paul would have liked to share that image with his father, but figured it would be disloyal.

They hadn't got into anything deep and it was better that way. Maybe they wouldn't have to. Maybe they could just share this visit as they shared the pleasure of being at a sunlit baseball game, pretending there had been no estrangement—that Paul had grown up and left home in the normal course of events and they merely happened to live in different cities.

Perhaps that was basically true, Paul thought—truer than he'd realized. His father had never preached or scolded or moralized and maybe Paul had been responsible for the disaffection—not because he intended to be but strictly because he had expected his conservative father to resent his own liberal attitudes and had reacted as if the man had when, in truth, he had not. Paul figured they could talk about that; indeed that was one of the things they *should* talk about.

When he'd told Harland he was going to Canada, Harland had said, simply, "Do what you feel is right." But it had not been that clear because Paul hadn't for a moment felt sure he was doing the right thing. He had felt like a lemming. He joined in a long line of his peers and marched into an uncertain sea. Jesus, he was glad he'd never grown his hair long. He'd never worn a sweatband around his forehead or begged, in a saffron robe, on the street corners. It wasn't much; it was something. Paul was proud of that.

He felt sure enough of himself to admit to whatever share of the guilt was his. What he didn't want to talk about was that goddamn letter he'd sent, for he was heartily ashamed of that self-pitying communication. He could not think what had caused him to write and send that letter. Oh, he knew the circumstances. There'd been a fight with Sarah and she'd stormed out, he was left alone to brood and there was a bottle of whiskey . . . yes, he could see why he wrote it, foolish as it was. If only he had not mailed it. If only the Canadian post office had lost it, as they did most letters. But he had sent it and it had been delivered and now he was dreading the moment his father mentioned it.

Maybe he wouldn't.

No, he would have to. It was the letter that had brought him here, how could he not mention it? Paul wondered how his father would do it. Would he preambled it in some round-about fashion, averting his gaze as he led up to the subject or would he look Paul right in the eye, man to man? It would be painful either way. Paul could imagine it. His father would gaze at him with sorrowful eyes, the sorrow magnified by his thick eyeglasses. Paul would look away. His father would say something that required an answer and Paul would mumble a reply and then, ashamed of his cowardice, he would raise his eyes and look directly at his father whereupon his father would falter and drop his own eyes, in turn. Their gaze would go up and down like a seesaw. Harland would look wise as an owl with those huge eyes but there would be no wisdom to be shared between them; they would share only embarrassment.

Well, first they would enjoy the game.

Paul hoped it would be a good game. That seemed important it more ways than the sport itself. He hoped that the home team would win. It was as if, by winning, they could prove Toronto a respectable city, Canada a big league country, a place where a man could live without shame—a place where Paul had chosen to go, instead of slinking off in cowardly confusion or being dragged there in the chains of fashionable behaviour, a slave to the spirit of his times and the mores of his age.

When the Blue Jays took the field, Paul cheered.

The game was ready to begin.

Both national anthems had been played and Sarah was not there to make fun of them when they stood facing the flag. They were seated in the colorful organge seats behind home plate. The stadium was filled to capacity on this pleasant day. Harl had a smudge of mustard on his lip; it seemed proper. The Blue Jay pitcher went to the mound and the Red Sox lead-off hitter came to the plate. Harland was looking around as if he might yet find a beer vendor lugging an illicit coolor up the aisle.

The batter grounded out on the first pitch.

Harland gave up his hopeless quest for a drink and began to watch the game with interest.

The second Boston batter struck out on five pitches.

The Boston line-up was fearsome but there were two outs and fans were clapping. The pitcher was throwing hard; the ball was really moving when it came in to the plate. He took a lead off first base. It brought up the venerable clean up hitter. The crowd was hushed.

Harland wiped the mustard from his lip. He did it casually; to Paul, it seemed portentous.

The pitcher threw a ball.

He threw a second ball. The crowd groaned. The hitter was poised like a statue, his bat held high. The pitcher stepped off the mound. He was young and blonde. He adjusted his hat. He threw a strike. The crowd was hushed. The hitter waited like doom, motionless and implacable. The pitcher shook off a sign from his catcher. He spat out tobacco. He threw a curve that didn't break and the batter stroked the ball with a solid whack. You could tell it was gone from the sound.

The ball left the infield like a cable strung to the fence, rising all the time. It cleared the fence to the right of the scoreboard, still rising. It cleared the small parking lot behind the fence and cleared the wire fence beyond that. It was a tremendous home run.

It came down in the gravel and bounced high against the wooden side of a wagon and rolled back under a caravan.

It was the longest home run ever hit in that stadium and the first time a ball had rolled under that caravan, where something else was waiting . . .

Chapter Twenty-Eight

Mike Ellis was ten years old and didn't have enough money to get into the ball park. He was playing catch with his friend Willy out behind the fence. He loved baseball. Willy loved baseball, too, but nobody loved it as much as Mike. He loved the solid thud when the ball went into the pocket of his glove. When Mike saw the home run ball clear the stadium his eyes lighted up and he said, "Jesus." Then, remembering that was a sin, he said, "Golly!" Mike had heard that they would let you into the park in exchange for a ball and he ran after it, intent on getting it before Willy did.

He saw the ball roll under a painted caravan.

He got down on his hands and knees and crawled in after it, reaching out in the shadows. He still had his baseball glove on and he reached out with his gloved hand first, because that was the way you stretched for a baseball in the dirt.

He touched something pliable.

He reached out with his bare hand.

He touched something soft and wet and squishy and, for a moment, Mike imagined that the ball had been struck so hard it had been mashed up like a rotten peach.

Then he got his head in under the wagon and saw what his hands were in.

Mike was a tough little kid and he didn't scream.

Chapter Twenty-Nine

Joe Greene had not been to the new zoo before and he didn't like it now.

He had liked the old zoo where you stood right in front of the cages and looked at the animals for as long as you liked. If the money threw shit at you who could blame him? The new zoo wasn't like that. It was so big that you couldn't walk around it and it wasn't the same, riding in a train, when you couldn't linger when and where you liked. He felt if he himself were caged in moving glass while the animals were free.

He regretted coming.

He regretted taking Bonny Cutter to the drive-in, too. That was stupid. He should have taken her to the restaurant. If you took a girl to a drive-in, she figured you wanted some nooky—at least a girl like Bonny did—and it had been an unfortunate evening. He didn't guess he'd call Bonny again. Maybe he would. How could you know what you were going to do?

Well, you knew what you were going to do if LaRoche told you to, of course. But sometimes you did things he hadn't told you to do, just the same. LaRoche had sent Greene around to the King Edward again but the witness—if witness he were—was still not in his room. The message that Greene had left was still in his box but that meant nothing except that he had not checked at the desk. He was probably not expecting any messages. He had not checked out, at any rate, and Greene had left a second message asking him to contact the police at Jarvis Street and then, on impulse—the same sort of impulse that had taken him to the library the previous day—had driven out to the zoo.

He wanted to look at a wolf.

He felt almost obsesed with wolves; felt that by just looking at a wolf he would know if he was right or wrong in his theory, as if the wolf would manifest the guilt of its species by flinching from his gaze just as a human suspect flinched when the rubber hoses came out.

But it was no good looking from the train.

They passed high above the wolf compound and the driver halted for a minute or two. Half a dozen wolves were visible. Two were romping like playful puppies. Greene couldn't look in their eyes from where he sat and he was glad when the train started moving again. They went past elephants like giant lumps of mud and buffalo like adobe walls in the light.

Greene went straight back to the parking lot, feeling a bit foolish for wasting his time. There was no way he was going to tell LaRoche where he'd been.

He was driving out the gates when the call came in from the stadium and he got it on his car radio.

Chapter Thirty

The Red Sox were leading ten to nothing and those thunderous bats had shattered Paul's mood as surely as they were destroying the Toronto pitching. It was depressing and it seemed in many ways symbolic. Paul and Harl decided to leave after the sixth inning.

They heard the sirens and saw the flashing lights as they walked down the ramp. They couldn't see what was happening. A yellow police car flashed past. On the side it said: TO SERVE AND PROTECT. To persecute and harass was what Sarah always said. Paul had said it a few times himself, just to be agreeable, and he knew he was supposed to scorn the police. But he never had. He even liked the idea that there were a few around if you needed them, although he had never admitted that to Sarah. Paul guessed he was pretty much a failure as a modern youth and hoped he would do better as a crotchety old man. He had no fear of aging, although he hoped he wouldn't have to wear thick eyeglasses the way his father did.

"Wonder what that's all about?" Harl said.

Paul didn't know.

"Why, what do I see there? Is that a tavern?"

It was. But it was just outside the stadium, whence they would still hear the dismal sounds of the slaughter and Paul said, "There's a better pub up the street."

They walked up to the Wheatsheaf for a beer.

"It wasn't much of a game, I'm afraid," Paul apologized.

They were sitting at a small, round table and the waiter brought draft beer on a tray.

"Oh, well," Harland said. "An expansion team . . . they'll get better. Bound to." He smiled. Then: "They really ought to sell beer, though at a baseball game." He said it as if that failure would explain or justify poor play but Paul knew he didn't really care about that; he was bitching about it instead of more serious things, using a blue-nosed law as a whipping boy. "Why, not selling beer . . . that's un-American," he added, grinning.

"We're in Canada," Paul said.

He said it seriously.

"Why, so we are. No wonder."

Sometimes it was hard to tell when his father was being tongue in cheek, Paul thought. At one point, yesterday, he had thought that Harland was actually being sardonic with Sarah. He hoped that was true. But it was hard to tell. Maybe it was the glasses. He wasn't poker faced, he had plenty of expressions . . . but you could never tell what they were expressing.

Paul took a deep breath and said, "Dad?" and when Harl looked at him he said, "I'm sorry about Sarah, Dad."

"Oh, if she doesn't like baseball . . ."

"No. I mean . . . I guess you don't think much of her . . ."

Harland said, "Awww," and gestured that it was not important.

"I can't blame you. But she's not always like she was yesterday; she's not always like that."

"Why, of course not. Certainly not. She's a woman." Harland surprised Paul by that. He was grinning, too, and it wasn't forced. "Who can ever tell about woman?"

"I guess," Paul said. Then: "I don't suppose that you ever had any word from Mom?"

Harland shook his head.

He still had the smile on his face but now, without any reason for being there, it seemed idiotic—a vestigal smile, lingering on to no purpose.

"I think maybe she'd dead, Dad."

"I've thought that," Harland said. He took his spectacles off and his eyes diminished.

Paul started to speak, then paused as the waiter came storming up, whipping their empty glasses away and slamming full ones down. He was an aged waiter, predating the liberalized laws, from a time when restrictions designed to limit drinking had forced immoderate gulping. He put two beers in front of each of them. Some foam sloshed from a glass and ran across the table onto Harland's spectacles, filming them like soapsuds. Harland lifted them, inspecting the lenses. As he moved them in and out before his face, his eyes seemed to rush forwards and then recede.

Paul had been dreading the moment his father mentioned the letter. Now, driven by some compulsion he did not understand, he brought the subject up himself.

"Dad, about that letter . . ."

"Barm," Harland said.

"What?"

"Barm. That's the word for the froth of a beer."

He smiled and wiped his eyeglasses on the edge of the tablecloth.

Paul, feeling helpless, said, "Oh. I didn't know that."

"Yes. That's what it's called. A brewer in a zymurg and the froth is barm. What about the letter?"

Paul felt disjointed and confused. The transistion baffled him. What about the letter. What had he intended to say? He could feel his face redden but he didn't know if his father could see it with his glasses off.

"Hell, what can I say? It was foolish . . ."

"You didn't sound happy," Harland said, a simple statement.

"I was in a bad mood. Morose. I'd been drinking. Hell, I was drunk as an owl. My life isn't so bad, not really bad at all. Honest, Dad . . . not bad . . ."

"Why, I didn't guess it was, Paul," said Harland. "People get moods, is all. I'm glad you thought to write to me, you felt the mood to write. To someone, I mean."

102

"I hope you didn't think I was . . . well . . ."

"It did depress me, Paul. The thing was, I didn't know what to do about it . . . what you wanted me to do . . ."

"I didn't want . . ."

" . . . so guess what I did? I went hunting. I haven't been hunting in ages, Paul; not since before you left . . . not since your mother left." He was smiling, his eyes unfocused, looking through time instead of distance. "It's strange, how things work out. Your mother never liked me to go off on a hunting trip. She resented it and she complained bitterly about it. But I liked to hunt and I went. That was the only real problem we had, your mother and I. I thought it was. Then after she left me and there was no one to object if I went, I didn't feel like it. Strange. How the mind works, I mean. There's a lot of strange linkage in the brain, Paul. Well, whatever . . . when I got your letter, I felt like hunting. I only went for one day. I'd sold my guns, you know and . . . anyhow, I got out in the woods for a day and then I felt more . . . resolved. I knew I had to come and see you, Paul . . . after I went hunting."

What is he saying? Paul wondered. Does it make sense?

Harland reached across the table and touched his son on the shoulder.

"But I didn't come to hassle you," he said. He was smiling again. "I just thought we could have a beer together . . ."

Paul felt a surge of relief, followed instantly by a welling up of joy and love for the man. He reached across the table and gripped Harland's bicep affectionately. His father's arm was like a bar of iron and with the glasses off he was a handsome man.

"Dad . . . thanks, Dad," Paul said.

Harland smiled diffidently and put his glasses on again.

They were still there when excited customers brought news of the murder and the waiter delivered it with the beer.

Chapter Thirty-One

They couldn't find the owner of the caravan and, after the police artists and photographers had worked on the scene, they decided to push the caravan off the body, rather than drag the body out, so as not to disturb its position. But even as they decided that, it seemed pointless. They'd all looked under the wagon and the body had been stuffed in there and what could they learn from that? They already knew that a warm corpse flops around, that arms and legs get contorted. None of them wanted to look at that body after it had been uncovered and it seemed gentler somehow to push the wagon off then drag the body out . . . get a hold on an arm or a leg and pull the dead girl out. Greene said, "Jesus . . . it would be just like a negative of what happened before . . . the killer stuffed her under there and pulling her out, well, it would be like it was a film running backwards. You know?''

Then he looked thoughtful.

"Or did she crawl under?"

"Is there a point to that statement?" LaRoche said. He was grim faced and tight as a bow string. His face had acquired a greenish tint.

Greene nodded slowly and doubtfully and said, "Maybe . . . maybe she saw . . . something . . . coming after her. She might have crawled underneath the caravan herself, trying to hide . . . and the killer crawled in after her . . ."

"Jesus! I hope not!"

They both had the same image. Their minds did not function in the same fashion as a rule but the same image came to both of them . . . the girl squirming back under the wagon, screaming or sobbing, terrified . . . hoping with final desperation that she would be safe there . . . and then something crawling in after her . . . .

"I hope not," LaRoche said again.

He signaled. Three uniformed policemen pushed the caravan forwards. They leaned into it, keeping their feet well back so that their momentum did not carry them too far. They didn't want to step on the corpse.

The caravan rolled off.

It had been sitting there for a long time and the wooden wheels had sunk into the earth and, moving, they pressed twin tracks up each side of the body. The girl's arm had been raised across her throat. As the rear of the caravan passed over, the bumber disturbed her elbow and as the corpse came into view the arm dropped to the side, the elbow stiff. The collarbone thrust up through torn flesh. It gleamed white. Splinters stuck up. Everyone could see that the collarbone had been chewed.

They looked.

And whether they knew it or not, everyone was very careful to keep his toes on his own side of the indentation that the rolling wheels had laid, that fragile border that kept them from the scene . . . that indented frame that separated them from the gruesome picture . . . .

Chapter Thirty-Two

"Who was she?"

LaRoche was speaking to the identification officer. Greene was with them.

"Christ, give me some time," the identification officer said. "What am I, a fucking computer? I look at a body, and the name and address pop out my asshole?"

LaRoche stared at him and when the officer dropped his eyes, said, "Sorry, Jim."

"Yeah. Didn't mean to snap, Steve. It's just . . . hell, I don't want to identify her. I will, but . . . I don't know; once you put a name on a body, it's more than just a body. It's a person, then. It lived and breathed . . . it had parents and friends and hopes and dreams . . . a future; a young girl like this one, she had a future, Steve. She probably had a boyfriend. Aw, you know.''

He lighted a cigarette.

He said, "Two cigarettes."

"What?"

"That's all she had on her. Two cigarettes in a box. No wallet, no identification. Probably too young to have a driver's license. Shit, she didn't even have any shoes. Two cigarettes and no shoes . . .''

"Maybe the killer took them," Greene said.

LaRoche looked at him in amazement. He was getting tired of Greene's theories. What did he think, for crissake? Did he think she'd been murdered by a shoe thief? Did he think a fucking foot fetishist did it? Or did he think a wolf carried them off, like a dog bringing carpet slippers to his master? But he didn't say that in front of the others.

"I doubt it," the identification officer said. He hadn't found the idea as unlikely as LaRoche had. "Lots of these kids walk around barefoot."

Greene, seeing the way that LaRoche looked at him, was thankful that Jim had taken the suggestion seriously enough to reply. He felt obligated to say something further.

He said, "What do you do next in a case like this, Jim? Fingerprints?"

Now the identification officer stared at Greene in amazement.

What the hell did I say now? Greene wondered.

"Fingerprints?" Jim said. "Fingerprints? Sure,

we take her fingerprints as a matter of course. But do you think we're gonna have a matching set on file? Do you suppose we got prints on every young girl in Canada? Maybe she wasn't Canadian. Maybe she'd never been arrested. You think she had a record? A young girl like that . . . or you think we fingerprint them at birth, as potential murder victims? Fingerprints are Sherlock Holmes crap, Joe. The public thinks they're magic, 'cause they work on television. But what the hell . . . the public will believe anything. They believe in twin blade razors and ten speed bikes, for crissake . . .''

"Sorry," Greene said, miffed.

The identification officer looked disgusted. He wasn't annoyed with Greene, his anger just flowed in that direction.

Speaking more softly, he said, "What I do first, I check the missing person reports."

And when he checked the report on Linda Drummond, he knew right away who the dead girl was. He had to check it out, but he knew.

"I thought she was shacked up," Jesse Drummond said. "I really did." He was desperately trying to convince his wife—and himself—of that. The full reality of Linda's death had not hit either of them yet. They both felt strangly empty, hollow, filled with a void into which, in time, the emotions would rush—nature delayed but inexorable in its abhorrence of a vacuum.

His wife nodded.

She was, if anything, more empty than her husband and she was thinking of Linda only indirectly.

I can divorce Jesse now, she was thinking.

But I can't. I can now, but I can't. How can I leave him alone with this . . . we've got to share this. And there was always some good reason why a woman got married . . . some good reason why she could not get divorced . . .

The police pathologist had tiny hands, a tiny mustache, and tiptoed about like a pantomine mouse, but his trade had immured him to sentiment. He was used to casting the runes of ruined bones and reading the portents in bloody bowels. To him she was not a victim—she was a sacrifice in which he could search for portents and decipher death.

He gave his preliminary report matter-of-factly.

But Greene was there and he hesitated at one point.

LaRoche said, "He knows."

The pathologist said, "I'll be able to tell you shortly; I'm having the saliva analyzed now. I'm assuming there will be the same . . . anomaly."

Then he spread his hands out and shrugged. He would report the facts; he had no opinions.

"All right," LaRoche said.

At the door, the pathologist turned back.

"Oh, one more thing," he said.

LaRoche and Greene waited.

"She wasn't interfered with."

They stared at him in awe.

He ventured a shy smile.

"Sexually, I mean, of course."

"Well, that's a good thing, isn't it?" said LaRoche.

"She was a virgin."

"Yes, I'm delighted to hear it."

The pathologist, detecting sarcasm, blinked. He was never sure of living emotions and could not pluck sarcasm out like a kidney from a corpse.

He turned and departed.

Chapter Thirty-Three

LaRoche was pouring coffee into a mug and looking tired about the eyes. It had been a long day. The initial impulse to act after the Dawson girl's body was discovered had ebbed with the drudgery of routine and then started again with the second murder. LaRoche felt used up. He felt as old as the earth.

LaRoche had met with the investigating detectives from both divisions, had been to see the Inspector twice and had been given what amounted to a pep talk by the Superintendent. He would much rather have walked the streets or driven about in a patrol car but that was not his job. His job was to head the homicide team from headquarters on Jarvis Street and now he had two homicides to deal with. But only one killer. It was evident that the same . . . man . . . had killed both girls.

It was going to be a longer day, too, and his wife would have to do without his presence at dinner once more.

It occurred to LaRoche that Stella, being Stella, might accidentally starve to death before this case was resolved; he simply could not imagine her actually cooking a meal and sitting down to eat it by herself.

He phoned her.

She said, "Oh, dear," not really complaining, when he told her he would be late.

Then she said an incredible thing.

"I just heard the news on the television, dear," she said. "Have you heard about these ghastly murders?"

LaRoche stared at the telephone for a moment.

Then he said, "I've been busy, darling; I don't have time to watch television."

"Of course not, dear," said Stella.

Now, pouring coffee, LaRoche said, "He killed the second girl too fast, Joe."

Greene was lost in thought and it took a moment before he understood what LaRoche had said. Greene had been thinking about the fact that Linda Drummond had been a virgin. When the pathologist had told them that, LaRoche had said, "Well, that a good thing, isn't it?" and Greene was wondering if it was a good thing. Did it matter? Was it laudable that her hymen was intact . . . when that was about the only part of her body that was? He had not the faintest idea, neither objectively nor subjectively. He wondered vaguely, what Bonny Cutter would have to say about a thing like that. But it was hard to imagine Bonny having ever been a virgin and he suddenly realized that his mind was wandering and that LaRoche had spoken.

At last, the words registered.

"Fast?" he said. "It didn't look to me like the poor kid died very fast, Steve."

LaRoche regarded Greene through the steam that was rising from his coffee cup. Now it seemed to be taking a long time for Greene's words to register.

He said, "No . . . no, I didn't mean that."

"That's what you said."

"He killed the second girl too soon after he killed the first, I mean. The Dawson girl was killed late the night before last or early yesterday morning . . . the Drummond girl sometime yesterday afternoon. The cycle is too quick. It isn't normal." He paused, realizing that normal was not quite the word he intended, although it certainly wasn't normal, at that. "Killers of this type have a schedule," he said. Now Greene stared at him, questioning that word. It made it sound as if the killer had been a train or something, running on time. And what was the killer? He wasn't a train . . . what was he? But he knew the word had been used objectively, and to the point. LaRoche went on: "How frequently did Jack the Ripper kill? Or the Boston Strangler? I don't think any madman has ever struck twice in the same day . . . not in unconnected circumstances I mean. It seems pretty well established that Dawson and Drummond didn't know each other. Not to any significant degree. Probably not at all.

There's no link between them. So that leaves us with . . . well, they were both young, both were pretty, both unfortunately happened to be alone in a deserted place. That's not enough. We need some tie-up between them, some pattern. And let's hope there is one, because if this bastard just kills at random then it's only by chance that we'll catch him, Joe. And he's killing too fast. Usually, with a guy like this, it builds up inside him, it reaches a crest and he kills . . . and then he's satisfied, he doesn't kill again until the same urge has had time to build up again. It's like . . . Christ, it must be like nicotine. The desire to kill must be just like a nicotine fit." He looked down into his coffee cup. "Or caffeine," he added.

"He isn't a sex fiend," Greene said, with some vague thought of Linda Drummond's virginity at the rim of his mind.

"It would appear not. There's no solid line of demarcation there . . . he may get a sexual thrill out of killing a girl . . . with his mouth."

That ugly thought brought a moment of silence.

Bonny Cutter had joked about cannibalism; Greene was pretty sure he wouldn't call Bonny again.

LaRoche said, "Suppose he keeps on. Suppose he kills one a day? At random. How do we predict when and where he will strike next?" He looked balefully at Greene. "The bastard isn't giving us time and we can't ask him for a time out."

"You think he might . . . kill again tonight? Tomorrow?"

"I don't know. It would be a pattern. One a day would be a nice, neat pattern."

Greene hated that thought.

"Both girls were blonde," he said.

LaRoche nodded; that meant little.

"Let's see . . . they were both sort of hippie types, I'd say."

That might well be more to the point; LaRoche nodded again.

"Both names . . . Dawson and Drummond . . . start with the letter D . . ."

LaRoche grinned. "You suppose he asked them their names? That coincidence, I think, would be too tenuous for MacMillan and Wife, Joe; Columbo would overlook that."

Greene grinned sheepishly. He guessed that he was getting pretty weary.

Then he plunged right in.

"What about the moon?"

LaRoche did not look scornful. Encouraged, Greene said, "The moon . . . I noticed last night . . . it's full. It's round, anyway. You know . . ." He almost used the word lycanthropy; he stopped himself in time; instead, he said, "Lunatics."

"That is . . . worth considering, I think."

"You do?" Greene was surprised.

"It's certainly advisable to get him before the next full moon. But that's true in any case. And I hope the newspapers don't get that idea. There's going to be some panic over this, as it is. If the public gets fed the idea that . . ." He didn't know how to finish that sentence. There were no words he chose to use there.

Greene said, "Is that why you're shying away from the idea that it could have been a wolf, Steve? Because it might cause greater panic?"

"Well, we don't want the guns to come out, Joe. Don't want every German Shepherd in town killed."

114

"Then you do think it might be a wolf?"

"I think nothing of the sort and I don't want anyone else thinking it, that's all I meant."

"But you checked with the zoo."

"It was no wolf, Joe."

"It was saliva from a wolf, dammit! You can't deny that."

"And there was human saliva, too; get things in the proper order in this mess."

"Yeah," Greene said.

He guessed LaRoche was right. His attitude was probably right. He watched LaRoche sip black coffee, the mug cradled in his hand and the steam coming up past his face. LaRoche still had ink on his thumb.

"Steve . . . I'd like to see this writer I mentioned. This Cronski. What harm could it do?"

"It could waste your time."

"I'll do it on my own time."

LaRoche looked at him hard and said, "You don't have your own time now, Joe; not now. Not until we get this guy. Joe . . . a man who writes books about wolves. A naturalist. Jesus, Joe. Why don't you do something useful, instead? Put a wig and a dress on and go for a walk in some dark place. That might do some good. Patrols and decoys, Joe . . . not interviews with writers."

Greene tugged at his lower lip, frustrated.

"I don't know much about wolves, Steve . . ." he said.

"I know about wolves," LaRoche said, surprising Greene.

Greene wondered if LaRoche had also gone to the library, despite his avowed skepticism? Even when he stated flat out that it couldn't have been a wolf, there was something . . . well, ambiguous in his attitude, something indefinite that hinted at more than a simple denial. It almost seemed as if LaRoche were afraid of the idea.

"Something about wolves," he said, pouring more coffee.

"I know they don't attack people," Greene said. "But I thought that in the case of a domesticated wolf . . . I don't mean that, exactly . . . a wolf that had been raised by humans or around humans . . . in captivity . . ."

"There were wolves where I grew up," said LaRoche, his voice strangely hollow so that it seemed to come out as an echo. "I saw my father chase a wolf pack off his trap line, once. They ran. He just bellowed at them and they ran away."

"Wild wolves. But . . ."

"And I saw a wolf-fight, once."

Greene sat on the edge of the desk, interested. LaRoche had never spoken much about his background. Now he said, "In a pit." Greene didn't know what he meant.

LaRoche said, "There was some dog-fighting up north. Sled dogs, mostly. Huskies. The owners would match their dogs for bets and it was a bloody business. Fascinating, though. Well, one fella showed up with a real fighting dog this one time. A pit bull. Squat as a log and belted with muscle . . . jaws like the gates of hell. Nobody ever seen a dog like that up there. He was matched with three of the best huskies, one after the other, and he killed them like that, one after the other, and wagged his tail for more. Quite a dog. Nobody cared to match a dog against the pit bull after that. It was just no contest; you could see he was going to kill any dog that got put in with him. Well, one

116

day a backwoodsman came in with a wolf. He'd caught it in one of his traps and he brought it in in a cage. It was a bitch, a mangy, half-starved, motheaten thing with a mangled foot. From the trap. Instead of shooting it, this backwoodsman figured to let the pit bull have some fun; he'd heard about it but he'd never seen it fight. Nobody bet on the match . . . it wasn't supposed to be a match, just some exercise for the pit bull. An execution. Everyone was quite merry about it. Festive. Well, they put the scrawny, cripped bitch wolf in the pit. It was terrified. A pitiful thing. It kept trying to jump over the wire mesh, to escape. Then they put the pit bull in. Well, the fighting dog knew its job and it went right after the wolf; the wolf tried to run away. It was frantic. The pit bull is wagging its tail, eager to fight; the wolf is whining. But there was no way for the wolf to get out of the pit; it turned and fought." LaRoche's voice was flat, his delivery casual; Greene was fascinated. "Joe, that mangy, under-nourished old bitch wolf tore the fighting dog to ribbons. The wolf would slash and back off, hoping the pit bull would quit. But pit bulls don't quit. They never quit. It just kept coming, trying to get the wolf in its jaws and the wolf just kept slashing and ripping and running. And, in the end, the wolf killed the fighting dog. It took a long time and an awful lot of blood but the wolf killed it in the end. In the pit." LaRoche's eyes were vague as he looked back through the years.

"Afterwards, they shot the wolf," he concluded.

Greene said nothing for some time as he tried to figure out the point of the story. The idea of fighting animals in a pit was repulsive to him but he knew that had nothing to do with why LaRoche had told the tale. It was something more than a moral judgment that was required.

He said, "Then you know how ferocious a wolf can be . . . you agree that . . .."

"Why, no," said LaRoche. "You missed the point. The wolf tried to escape, that was the point; don't matter that it killed the fighting dog, it tried to run away before it fought. Those girls weren't in a pit."

"Oh," said Greene.

And then LaRoche surprised him.

"All right," he said. "Go see your wolf expert."

"Thanks, Steve," Greene said, and he left before LaRoche had a chance to change his mind. LaRoche shook his head and poured some more coffee. He was getting caffeine nerves and his hand shook on the mug. The killer's hands probably shook just like that when he was getting the urge to kill. But he was killing too fast; he'd be shaking all the time . . . he'd be a walking avalanche. LaRoche sat at his desk and remembered other things he had heard in the northern wilderness; things he didn't really want to remember. He had believed them, then, but he had been a child. Now he was a cop and he couldn't believe that sort of stuff . . . but he thought about it and his hands trembled.

Chapter Thirty-Four

Paul had been worried about Sarah and kept glancing at his watch but when Harland noticed this and suggested that Paul should be getting home, Paul felt compelled to say, "Aw, there's no hurry; let's stop somewhere else." So they'd called in at a sequence of pubs and bars and it was getting late by the time Harland stopped the car outside the apartment building. He stayed behind the wheel with the motor running and both hands still on the wheel. He was tapping the rim with his index finger. Paul knew he was waiting to be asked up for a beer.

Paul said, "It's terrible . . . those murders."

"It certainly is."

Paul nodded. They agreed on some things. But they'd already talked about the murders and he figured it was pretty silly to continue. He had to either invite his father in or say good night and get out of the car. He couldn't decide which to do; he didn't know which his father wanted him to do, either. Harland would accept an invitation for a nightcap and probably expected one, but that might well be through convention rather than desire. They'd already had plenty to drink.

Harland's finger tapped, tapped, tapped.

Paul wondered if Sarah was home. He hoped not because he figured she would be in a sullen mood and probably would make things unpleasant. She would have been simmering all day; his arrival would add the heat of fusion to her temper. On the other hand, if she weren't home, he'd have to explain her absence to his father and that would be embarrassing. He'd have to wonder where the hell she was, too. Sarah was not the most chaste of girls. In fact, she was a tramp. It was a quality that she deliberately cultivated, which didn't make it any better. She wasn't a nymphomaniac; it was just that she slept around to prove that she was liberated and uninhibited. She feigned unbridled passion. Nor did it help that she didn't expect fidelity from Paul. Paul was faithful by nature and Sarah laughed scornfully at such an outmoded concept. When he passed up a chance to sleep with another woman, Sarah called him a good soldier.

"Well," Harland said.

He tapped the wheel.

Paul knew that his father had always been faithful to his mother. Whatever had ruined their marriage, it had not been another woman. Even after she left, Harland had not looked for another woman. Paul guessed that he had inherited his own tendency towards monogamy. He didn't regret it.

"Well," said Harland. He said it several times.

Aw, shit, Paul thought.

"Want to come up for a beer, Dad?" he asked.

"Why, that's an idea!" said his father.

Paul was not sure if he wanted Sarah to be home, where she would no doubt be obnoxious to his father, or out, where she would no doubt be coupling with some bearded freak.

As it turned out, he got the worst of both options.

She was home, but just on her way out, when Paul and Harland came into the shabby flat.

"Have a nice hot dog, did you?" she sneered.

She was wearing a light cotton dress. Her nipples could be seen in little peaks against the material.

120

Paul didn't want to argue with her.

"Sorry, we're late," he said.

She shrugged.

He said, "There's been another murder . . . just behind the baseball stadium . . ."

"Oh, how exciting," she said.

She still wished she had gone with them. Unable to admit that, she was furious with the whole situation. She didn't really feel like going out, either. But she had to.

"It must have made your day," she said.

Harland looked embarrassed.

Paul said, "Sarah, for crissake. What kind of thing is that to sasy? A girl was murdered . . ."

"Yeah. That makes two. Big deal. How many Vietnamese children were killed, Paul? Bombs and napalm. You don't seem to care about them . . . so what's this concern with a couple murders here? Ummm? Can't you put your head in the sand when it happens where you live?" She stuck her jaw out belligerently. Paul was astounded; this attack was so ridiculous that he could not resent it. He felt like laughing in her face. "Who cares? Except the newspapers who'll capitalize with juicy headlines."

"Well, now . . ." Harland said, but he faltered as she shot him a black look.

She waited, looking back and forth between them; the fact that neither of them chose to argue with her served to increase her annoyance.

"I'm going out," she said.

"Okay," Paul said.

She hesitated, waiting for him to ask where she was going or, better yet, tell her he didn't want her to go, so that she could tell him it was none of his business.

121

Paul understood this. So he said, "Where are you going?" just to be predictable.

"Out," she said.

"Well . . . will you be back soon . . . or . . .?"

"What's it to you? I'm not a doll, am I? You can't keep me in a box and take me out when you want to."

"Oh, for crissake, Sarah . . ."

"You'd like that, wouldn't you? One of these blow up dolls you could inflate when you wanted a piece of ass?"

Harland looked shocked.

Noting that, Sarah felt smug.

She shrugged and went out. She left the door open. They could hear her heels click and clack down the stairs.

Paul was greatly ashamed.

He said, "She's got all these damned hang-ups . . ."

He closed the door. It did not fit nicely into the frame; a door that would not properly shut her out and seal his father and Paul off from reality.

"She's not really like that . . . not all the time. I guess she's just in a bad mood . . ."

Harland said nothing. Paul went to the cooler and took out two bottles of beer. He snapped them open. Harland took his hat off. He held it in one hand and took the beer in the other. For a moment he looked confused, as if he couldn't decide which hand to raise to his mouth.

"Don't let it bother you," Paul said.

"Why, no . . . it's none of my concern."

Then Harland grinned and surprised Paul; he said, "A rubber doll, huh? Ain't that something? What a thing to say!"

They both laughed. They felt better.

"You going to marry the girl?" Harland asked. He was still grinning when he said it so that it didn't seem to make much sense to Paul.

Paul gestured, not quite a shrug. "No," he said.

"Um. Going to stay with her?"

"Why . . . you know . . ." Paul paused and took a slug of beer. He had not the faintest idea what he meant to say.

Then he said, "No," and the moment he said it, he realized, for the first time, that it was true.

Chapter Thirty-Five

N.V. Cronski was a woman, a fact which totally surprised Sergeant Joe Greene when he met her. His surprise amused her. She lived in Rosedale, in a house like a fortress with walls of gray stone and a front door so huge that it seemed to require a drawbridge to see it off properly.

She answered the door herself. She was a small, slender woman. Greene felt small himself framed in the arch of those massive portals.

He asked for Mr. Cronski.

She smiled and said, "There is no Mr. Cronski," and let him wait for a moment before she said, "No doubt you mean N.V. Cronski, yes?"

Greene nodded.

"I am Cronski."

"Oh," said Greene.

There was a sort of foreign charm and graceful confidence about the woman. Greene introduced himself and showed his identification. She was neither alarmed nor surprised.

"Of course," she said. "Come in."

Greene followed her down a vaulted corridor and into a large chamber which looked more like a church than a room. Sections of the walls were bare stone, other segments were panelled in oak; there was a huge fireplace and hearth. Somehow, the room looked wrong to Greene but he couldn't say why that was, at first. Then he realized that the patterns of light and shade seemed random—broad, irregular blocks of adumbration seemed to lie on the walls without reason, as if the shadows lurked there by whimsy, and the odd shapes of illumination were cast by no visible source. Greene felt uncomfortable in such a room. Maybe it was more like a luxurious dungeon than a church, he thought; he would not have been unduly startled to find torture devices squatting in the shadows or starving wretches chained to the walls. He grinned at that fancy but he had gulped a couple of times as he followed Cronski into the room.

Although his heavy shoes were loud on the floor, she made no sound at all.

He saw that she was barefoot.

Then he could barely see her at all.

She was dressed in black; as she moved through an oblong of shadow she almost disappeared. Then she stepped into the light again; she was motioning him to a chair. He sat on the very edge, balanced as if ready to spring up again at any moment.

"And what can I do for the minions of the law?" she said, smiling in an amused and tolerant fashion, as she might have to a child. He had a sensation of wisdom coming from her, or a sense of time passed. But she was not very old, he thought; and she was attractive. Her face was triangular, her eyes tilted, her hair dark and long and straight.

Greene excused himself for troubling her; she accepted his apology with a slight shift of her shoulder.

"If this is an inconvenient time . . .?"

"Please."

Greene leaned forward.

"Wolves," he said.

"Certainly."

Greene was taken aback.

"What else?" she said. "That is my field."

"Yes," he said. He watched a shadow change shape on the wall behind her. It didn't flicker as if the light were drifting; it simply moved in a block a few inches to the side. He could see neither the source of the light nor the shape that blocked that shadow.

He said, "You've heard about the murders?"

"There was a girl killed . . ."

"And another this afternoon . . . that is, the body was discovered this afternoon."

"I see."

"Another girl killed in the same fashion,"

Greene said. He wasn't sure how much he should tell her. He felt out of control in this strange room with her level gray gaze upon him, felt as if there had been a slight shift in reality, as if his perceptions were changing without reason, like the shadows. He couldn't think of what to say next.

Cronski said, "And you believe a wolf responsible?"

"Well . . . not exactly . . . not definitely . . . I mean, in your opinion, could a wolf be loose in Toronto?"

"Certainly," she said, without pausing to consider it.

"Would it kill?"

Now she paused; instead of replying, she said, "What makes you think it was a wolf?"

Greene suddenly felt as if he were being interrogated; it made him feel sorry for criminals.

He said, "There were certain indications," and that was all he intended to say but she was waiting for him to elucidate. He felt as if she were physically dragging words from him. But it was ridiculous. He was supposed to be asking the questions, he knew procedure and method; he tightened his face and said, "Just certain indications, no definite; I merely wanted your opinion."

"A wolf might well survive in a city," she said. She turned a hand over in a gesture he could not define. "They are adept at hiding; if seen in a city, a wolf would undoubtedly be mistaken for an Alsatian or German shepherd. But that is hardly the point. Why would a wolf come into the city? That is most unlikely."

"I was thinking more of . . . well, if a wolf escaped from the zoo, or were turned loose . . ."

"Has a wolf escaped?"

"Not that we know of."

"But why would he stay? A wolf would head directly for the wilderness."

"Even one born in captivity? A pet, say?"

"Instinct, I think . . . I am sure . . . would prove stronger than environment, in any case. I have, in fact, raised wolves myself. Freed, they invariably fled. They do not flee from me, you must understand. They . . . regarded me with affection. I am . . ." she smiled . . . "I am sympathetic towards wolves. No, they left me with regret . . . but the wilderness called too strongly. The classic call of the wild . . ."

Greene nodded. He was learning nothing new here, nothing he had not read at the library.

"But suppose, for some reason, a wolf did stay . . . would it kill?"

"No," she said, quickly.

That was so unequivocal that Greene blinked.

He said, "I know there are no recorded cases . . . possibly among the Indians, in the past . . ."

"In a pack, driven by famine . . . even then, I doubt it. Even in their own element, I doubt it. And in a city, an alien sphere . . ." She turned her face away, staring at the walls. In profile, the tilt of her eyes were more noticeable. Greene wondered what her ancestry was. Not looking at him, she said, "Were either of the victims . . . devoured?"

Greene shook his head but, not looking at him, she didn't see the negations he said, "No. They were . . ." he hesitated because he was not supposed to tell anyone the gruesome details—and yet he was seeking her advice and how could she give that without knowing the facts? He said, "Both girls had been . . . chewed. But not eaten.''

Greene winced at his own words but Cronski did not appear to find his statement distasteful.

''Well, that should answer your question . . . one question, at least. If the wolf were not mad with hunger, why would it kill? Surely this . . . these . . . girls did not attack it. Threaten it? It was not acting through self-preservation. So the wolf had no reason to kill, no motive, you see.'' She turned back to him and smiled. ''An unlikely suspect, Sergeant.''

''Yes.''

''And what are you keeping from me, in that case?'' she said, quite abruptly.

''Oh, nothing . . . we just thought . . . we are simply covering all the possibilities. . .''

''I am not a fool, Sergeant Greene.''

Greene blinked.

''The victims were . . . chewed, as you put it. The marks left by the fangs of a wolf and not indistinct, you know. Yes, of course you know. What have your forensic laboratories discovered? Why are you here?''

Greene tried to look stern. Then he realized that his head was wobbling a bit. He was perched on the very edge of the chair. He said, ''The facts are . . . well, I am not allowed to reveal any further details.''

''Then of what value are my opinions? You are wasting me time, Sergeant. Not knowing the facts . . .''

''I'm sorry. I just.''

''You shall have my opinions,'' she said.

Her eyes had narrowed; her triangular face seemed to have flushed without actually changing color, as if she controlled the shadows of her visage. She said, "It is my opinion—and a fact, as well—that the wolf has been sadly maligned through the ages. It has been persecuted and driven towards extinction. Even the commonplace image of the wolf is wrong. The cunning wolf, the efficient predator . . . nothing could be further from the truth." She spoke with passion and conviction. "The wolf, Sergeant, is a most inefficient hunter. That is why it is so vital to the balance of nature. A wolf does not kill a healthy animal. It cannot. It is neither fast enough or strong enough. The wolf takes the aging, the sick, the malformed . . . and strengthens the species on which it preys."

Greene was nodding, agreeing with her, feeling foolish as she lectured him.

"They eat mice," she said.

"Yes. I read . . ."

"I personally feel far more affection towards wolves than human beings," she added. She smiled. "A quirk of my nature, perhaps; an aberration. I think not. If a wolf killed a person, I should feel no deep regret . . . except for the further persecution that would result. If it were believed that a wolf were responsible for these deaths, wolves would be butchered out of hand. And it is not possible."

Greene held his hand up, palm out, as if to ward off her rising anger.

"That is why we want to keep it quiet," he said, bordering the truth.

She let out a deep breath. It hissed, like a safety valve on her emotions. He wishes he could explain to her about the saliva. Would LaRoche let him do that? He scraped his feet on the floor for a moment, as if scratching for purchase, then impulsively stood up.

"Thank you for your time," he said.

She was no longer angry; she said, "Then there is nothing more you wish to ask me?"

Greene started to speak, then stopped.

He couldn't ask her about . . . the other things.

His mouth was open; he had to say something. He said, "I read one of your books."

"Ah?"

He shrugged and said, "Thank you," again.

"It was nothing. I could, perhaps, have been more."

Greene turned on his heel and walked through blocks of light and slabs of shadow to the door.

Then he turned and walked back.

Cronski smiled, as if anticipating his words.

Greene was still telling himself that he must not mention it—even as he did.

"What do you think about werewolves?" he asked.

He blushed as he spoke, expecting her to laugh at him. She didn't laugh. Her eyes gleamed but not with laughter.

"That," she said, "is a different matter . . ."

Chapter Thirty-Six

Sarah Carlyl sat at the bar in the Jamacia Tavern, drinking a mug of beer and wishing she hadn't gone out. She was neither as liberal nor as loose as she liked Paul to believe and was often more bored than she cared to admit. It was a bore to get picked up by strange men. But she felt that she couldn't let Paul know she was reasonably faithful and she feigned nymphomania because it was fashionable, in much the same way that Paul had fled the draft. The birth control pill had liberated some women against their natures and Sarah was helplessly locked into her generation.

She crossed her legs and nursed her beer.

She didn't like the Jamaica. But it was the nearest bar to the apartment and she didn't like to walk far. The bar was circular and topped with formica; the room stretched back, long and narrow, beyond the bar and there were topless go-go dancers on a sequence of platforms, reflected again and again in mirrors down the walls. There were four girls but their images shot back and forth so it seemed there were dozens of them gyrating and squirming up and down the room.

Exploitation, Sarah thought.

Dumb girls flopping their boobs around while toothless old men gaped at them. Sarah thought is disgusting, no better than if they had been posed on an auction block, indentured for meager wages, slaves to old men's eyes.

She crossed her legs the other way.

A man stood beside her. There were plenty of

empty seats but he got right up close to Sarah. She knew that her nipples pushed out against her dress.

"Buy you a drink?" he asked.

She shook her head.

"Don't like a good time?" he asked.

"Your dick's too small," she said. That had been a stroke of genuis, she thought, pleased with herself; she had sounded properly lewd without being available. The man looked stricken. He walked out without having a drink. Sarah felt wicked and clever. Then a girl in a very short skirt came in, looked around and slide onto the stool next to Sarah.

She had frizzy hair and looked a lot like Little Ophan Annie. The bartender came down, whisking the damp counter with a damp rag. He was sweating. He wiped his brow with the same rag and said, "What'll it be, Rosy? The usual?"

The girl nodded. She was chewing gum. The bardender mixed a rye and coke. He put it in front of her.

How could a girl be a regular in a place like this? Sarah wondered. She must be a go-go dancer on her break.

Sarah saw that Rosy was staring at her speculatively. Sarah smiled faintly and looked away. Then she looked back. Rosy's jaw went up and down on the chewing gum; she sipped her drink, the gum pushed out of the way by her tongue.

"You working?" Rosy asked.

"Pardon me?"

"You working?"

"Working? Now, you mean?" Sarah said. She had a horrible thought that Rosy had mistaken her for one of the exploited go-go dancers.

"I mean, are you a working girl?" Rosy said. She chewed gum, she sipped rye and coke, chewed some more. She said, "Naw, I guess not. You don't know what I mean, I guess you ain't." She grinned. "A whore."

"What?" Sarah asked, amazed.

Sarah was tremendously embarrassed to realize that she was embarrassed; she was blushing.

Rosy said, "Nothing to be ashamed of, you are. I'm a working girl myself. Work out of this dump, most of the time; work the streets some, too. Why I asked, most girls that get in here on their own, they're in on the game."

"I didn't know . . ." Sarah was confused. She hated herself for blushing. She had no idea if whoring was liberated or not, if a whore was being exploited or was exploiting men, and when she couldn't place a thing within a proper framework she always got confused.

She smiled weakly and got up.

Rosy watched her, massaging the gum stoically.

Sarah left without finishing her beer.

Stuck-up bitch. Rosy thought.

She looked around for clients, brutalizing the gum for all she was worth.

Sarah was shocked—not because she'd met a whore or because she'd been mistaken for a whore, but simply because the meeting had shocked her—she was shocked at being shocked. It wasn't cool. For some reason, it made her feel sorry that she'd been so bitchy to Paul and his father. His father probably had to go to prostitutes, she reflected, being middle-aged and having those big, staring eyes like an owl, and it wouldn't have hurt her to be civil to him.

She walked back towards the apartment building.

She'd been out long enough to save face and she was thinking that if Paul's father was still there she would be pleasant; she would offer to make coffee or something; maybe she would tell them that she had been mistaken for a whore, that ought to be good for a few laughs. She wouldn't let on it had shocked her, she'd make it amusing.

She went into the dark hallway and walked down towards the stairs. The light was out. She wished that the landlord would replace the bulb; she wished that she hadn't gone out; she wished that life were less boring and that she could be a nicer person . . . .

Chapter Thirty-Seven

He still retained thought processes but they had degenerated as instinct took control. His human mind was there but it was blurred by a savage, throbbing sensation. His senses had been sharpened by the dulling of his mind.

He could hear her coming from a long way off. He could smell her, too, and hear her breathing. His nostrils flared and his lips were back from his teeth. She was closer. Her footsteps were as loud as drums and beneath that pounding he could hear softer sounds—he could hear her blood pulse in her veins and her pulse flutter in her throat.

The tendons tightened up his forearms, dragging his hands into hooks. His eyes gathered the feeble light that penetrated under the stairs, shining in the darkness. She was very close. Bang, bang, bang, her feet came down, punctuating her approach and she was so close now that the living warmth of her body wafted over him, compelling, demanding, drawing him out.

He could hear her heart beat.

He came out from under the stairs.

Sarah had started up the staircase; she paused on the second step as she heard the labored breathing and half-turned, looking down. She saw his eyes, bright in the darkness.

Her mouth opened but if she screamed, he did not hear her, for his ears were rushing to the rhythm of her blood.

She stepped backwards, her face tilted back and her mouth open. He could see her soft throat vibrate silently;, he heard her very impulses leap and spark.

Sarah turned, whirling; she mounted three steps before his hand closed on her ankle and he drew her back. She fell forwards, up the stairs, as he drew her back by the ankle. She hit her head on the steps. Dazed, she clawed at the rubber mat on the stairs, trying to pull herself up and away from him as he pulled her, step by step, back to his panting lust.

She was face down.

He turned her over, slowly.

Then she was face up, still trying to scream, as his face came down.

He did not hear her scream.

For a long while he heard only bubbling noises.

Chapter Thirty-Eight

A man named Smith had driven into Toronto two weeks before. He came from Buffalo and had heard that Toronto was jammed with lewd women and had come up to try his luck. Crusing up Yonge Street he got excited by the neon and the strolling girls. He turned into a sidestreet to park his car and punctured a tire on a broken beer bottle. That, he thought, was a pain in the ass. That was just his luck. Muttering and cursing, he jacked the car up and put the spare wheel on. He skinned his knuckles. All he needed was a flat tire when there were lewd women waiting. He put the jack back in the trunk, decided the car was parked well enough and hurried on towards the bright lights and the loud music. In his haste to sin, he forgot about the punctured tire which was leaning against the side of the car. Later, drunk, he lost his wallet and never did find a girl; disillusioned, he returned to his car and drove off, sick and disgusted, forgetting the tire which rolled away from the side of the moving car and flopped, deflated, on the sidewalk. Later, someone rolled it into a alley. The tire was still in the alley, the alley was beside Sarah's apartment building, and Gary Pearsall's head was resting on the tire.

Gary was stoned.

He'd been drinking and smoking and somehow he had wobbled into the alley, probably to take a leak, and he'd passed out. Now he woke up with his head on the ruptured tire and dogshit on his elbow.

He woke because he heard Sarah's broken, bubbling cry.

Gary staggered to his feet, shivering with cold and vague about where he was. He leaned against the wall and groaned. He sort of remembered hearing a scream but he wasn't at all sure that it hadn't been his outraged conscience.

After a few minutes he stumbled out of the alley . . . and something else came out of the doorway.

Gary stood very still.

The bulky shape moved right past him, so close

137

he could have reached out and touched it—but Gary had no desire whatsoever to touch something like that. He turned, rigid, like a post pivoting in the ground; he looked after the figure. He saw that the head was down and the shoulders were hunched up and he saw one hand, hooked and hanging—and from the fingers of that hand, dark, sluggish drops were falling to the ground.

Gary entered the front door of the apartment building three times and came back out three times, without advancing beyond the doorway. Vague with drink and awed by what he'd seen, he couldn't make up his mind what he should do. He didn't want anything to do with the cops, who often arrested him for insignificant and meager reasons, and he didn't want to know what had uttered that bubbling cry, but he couldn't seem to get himself together enough to walk away from it.

The dark entrance drew him to it.

One the fourth attempt he managed to go in just far enough to see the body broken at the foot of the stairs. Although the hallway was dark, Gary could see the body clearly in a terrible chiaroscuro —her limbs were white. Gary was trembling. He had to lean against the wall for a moment, afraid that his legs were going to fail him. The wall was wet. Gary shuddered. He got his cigarette lighter out and held it before him. For a long time he didn't strike it; he was holding it out in front of him as he might have held a crucifix in the face of a vampire. His thumb was on the wheel and his hand was shaking.

Then he spun the wheel and the flame shot up.

The scene zoomed into his sight.

The girl's arms and legs were at abrupt angles

138

and, although the body was on its back, the head had been turned around so that her chin rested on the first step, as if she had been gazing up towards safety at the top of the stairs. She had been dragged back, clawing, from that safety; her fingernails had parted the black rubber mat in parallel furrows from step to step. The furrows glistened like the tracks of a snail. Back from the floor of the stairs the blood had splayed out along the wall, like red fingers reaching for him.

He knew why his shoulder was wet.

Gary turned and went back out and he was already on the sidewalk before he realized that he was still holding the cigarette lighter like a beacon in front of him, following the dancing light down the street. At the corner he found a phone booth. He called the police. They were very attentive. Gary refused to give his name and he had every intention of leaving before they arrived on the scene, but after he hung up he vomited all over the telephone and then just stood there in the booth, too weak to move. He was still there when the police arrived.

They had come very quickly.

The police treated Gary much better than he had expected or was accustomed to. They were polite, called him "sir," and made no reference to the vomit on the front of his shirt or the dog shit on his elbow. They did take note of the blood on his shoulder, not mentioning it but looking at one another with meaningful glances. But after they had a look in the hallway, they understood.

One of the cops vomited, too.

They had gone in with flashlights and Gary vaguely wondered if it looked worse in the bright electric illumination, with all the details clear—or maybe not quite as bad as it had been in the uncertain flame of his cigarette lighter. They asked him to sit in the back of the police car and they used the radio. Gary had no idea how long he waited there. It wasn't long but for Gary time was suspended. He had a cigarette in his mouth but it was not lighted. He couldn't find a match and he simply could not bring himself to strike his cigarette lighter. He thought he might never use it again.

Gary realized that there were a great many yellow cars there now, with flashing lights; people went in and out of the building. Gary wondered if they had forgot him. He wanted to smoke. After awhile a man came over and got in the back seat with Gary.

"LaRoche," he said.

"Got a light?" said Gary.

LaRoche gave him a light. In the flare, Gary could see that the cop was unshaven and tousled and bleary-eyed—yet he looked like a man who should be crisp and neat and sharp. Gary inhaled deeply.

"Do you live in the building?" LaRoche asked.

Gary shook his head.

"How did you come to be there?" LaRoche asked. He wasn't being intimidating.

"I was just . . . passing by," Gary said, near enough to the truth. He didn't want to mention that he had been passed out in the alley, although he could see that this cop wasn't going to arrest him for vagrancy or public intoxication. Still, he

140

had his pride. He said, "Walking past . . . I heard a scream. Then this weird guy came out . . ."

LaRoche lighted a cigarette himself then.

"Can you describe him?"

"Yes . . . no . . . I mean, sort of . . ."

LaRoche didn't want to listen to another description but he had to. He stared at Gary. They were both smoking and they had fallen into a pattern, inhaling alternatively, so that Gary's face flared up, then LaRoche's face lighted in turn. There seemed a terrible intimacy between them as they leaned towards each other in the back of the car.

"There was blood on his face . . . his mouth," Gary said. He was trying to remember. He was sober now, cold sober, but he'd been drunk when he saw the man and his memory was blurred. Had there really been blood on his mouth? Jesus. He thought there really had been. "He was kind of hunched up. After he went by I saw one of his hands. I remember his hand better than his face. I don't know why . . ." he said, but actually he did; he'd been drunk when he saw that face and instantly sober as it moved on. He shuddered. LaRoche waited patiently. "It was like . . . I don't know . . . like a flower, maybe. Yeah, like a red flower, with the fingers like petals, half-closed and . . . dripping . . ."

LaRoche was nodding. His face was constricted. He said, "But it was a man?"

Gary didn't understand.

"It was . . . human?"

"Well, yeah . . . It was a guy, all right."

Gary thought that had been a funny question

141

and he noticed that LaRoche sighed—almost as if such an obvious answer had brought him satisfaction . . . .

Like solid white pillars, the electric torch beams crisscrossed down the street. Then they stopped and moved around in one place, intersecting and diverging.

Then they came back.

One of the uniformed cops approached LaRoche, lowering his light as he came. His head was lowered as well. "The blood stops before the corner," he said. "Maybe in daylight . . ."

LaRoche nodded and waved him away. LaRoche was standing in the doorway; down by the stairs the police artists were at work and the fingerprint men were dusting the walls, working carefully around the banners of blood. LaRoche passed a hand across his brow. He was exhausted. He couldn't seem to think, he couldn't focus, even his wrist was limp as he dragged his hand over his forehead.

But the killer had been human!

Pearsall had not equivocated about that, the way Ike Clanton had. It was something. Maybe it would shut Greene up on his damned wolf theory.

Where the hell was Greene, anyhow?

Oh, yeah . . . so tired he'd forgotten . . . Greene had gone to have a sociable chat with his wolf expert. LaRoche was suddenly furious with Greene . . wasting time while another girl was killed! Then his anger vanished as abruptly as it had come over him. No matter where Greene had been, he wouldn't have been in that dark hallway, anyhow, would he? There was no sense in taking it out on Greene, that terrible frustration . . . .

The younger of the two police artists were also frustrated. His name was Dublin and he lived a life of constant frustration, painting in oil in his spare time and never selling anything and earning his living by drawing corpses.

He felt like a whore.

When he'd first started the police work he had rationalized it away by telling himself that Leonardo Da Vinci had sketched plenty of dead bodies in his notebooks, studying the flayed cadavers to learn the way the body worked; how it was jointed and muscled and structured. But the time for rationalization was past, now . . . and that broken body defied the rules of anatomy. The parts were in the wrong place, the joints were out, the angles were wrong.

When they had finished, the two artists went out past LaRoche and stood on the sidewalk, smoking.

They were both glad to be out of the hallway—but there were drops of blood on the sidewalk, too.

If he had been working in oil, Dublin thought, he would have used burnt sienna for the blood. He walked around a bit. The other artist was older and Dublin thought him dull; he never talked of aesthetics and had no ambition. He stood in one place while Dublin walked back and forth. Dublin would have used a palette knife to get the right texture of the walls . . . burnt sienna, nice and thick and spread out with deft, sure strokes. He wondered if it was sick to think that way.

He wandered out into the road and looked up at

the old tenement. He was willing to bet there was a loft at the top, maybe even a starving artist. He wandered back. His partner was lighting another cigarette from the butt of his first.

"You know what?" Dublin said.

"What?"

"It was like a Picasso."

"What?"

"The body. It was out of perspective, like a Picasso."

His partner stared at him with dull eyes.

"Know what I mean?"

"Naw."

Dublin gestured, frustrated. He was an artist and he knew that an artist had trouble with verbal communication. He could paint what he meant but it was hard to say it.

He said, "Disjointed . . . flawed by design . . . fixed in a statis . . ." He was using the words he felt but could only vaguely define and the older man was staring incredulously at him. "Anamorphic . . . all the elements were there, the body would have looked normal, viewed in the proper perspective . . ."

"What kind of crap is that?" said the older artist.

"Just like a Picasso," said Dublin.

Chapter Thirty-Nine

There was some sort of commotion in the street and Paul James could see flashing lights in the window pane. They showed how grimy the glass was. He was lying on the mattress but he hadn't been sleeping. Sarah had not come home yet and he was waiting and wondering if she would. He guessed she would. But he wished that she'd got home before his father left. Harland had seemed quite concerned that she was still out by the time he'd gone, although he hadn't stayed long. He'd had the one beer and he'd asked Paul if Sarah often stayed out late—but not all night, he didn't ask that although he was obviously thinking it—and where on earth she might have gone. But he was casual about it; he hadn't preached and he hadn't hassled. Paul had shrugged off her absence as if it were nothing, muttering something about visiting friends. But it was something, at that. It was none of his father's business but it was something to Paul.

Now Paul got up and moved to the window.

There were police cars in the streets and that was none of Paul's business . . . except that he lived in the neighborhood where such things happened.

He rubbed his forefinger down the glass. It came away grimy and the clear line he had drawn flashed brighter when the lights hit it. Sometimes Paul felt that his mind was coated with grime, too, that he could not see things clearly through the dust. He thought that he would wash the windows in the morning, if Sarah didn't come home. Not if she did—she'd laugh at him for that. But maybe he wouldn't bother. What was the point? What was there to see?

Paul felt no curiosity about the police cars.

He was glad it had nothing to do with him . . . .

Chapter Forty

When LaRoche finally got home, Stella was fast asleep; when he awoke in the morning she was already up and brought him coffee in bed. His sleep had been disrupted by dreams. Awake, he could not remember them but the impressions lingered along with his coffee, haunting moods and eerie, vague images that had slipped through his slumber.

Stella sat on the edge of the bed.

Christ! He hoped she didn't want sex.

He was still tired and he was trying hard to recall

the details of his dreams and Stella said, "Poor dear," for she saw that he was overworked and disturbed.

Then she said, "Will you be home for lunch, darling?"

"I don't think so."

"Oh, dear."

"Stella, I . . ."

"I understand, dear," she said.

He guessed that, in her vague way, she did. He thought that maybe he should make love to her. But she got up and moved away from the bed; LaRoche finished his coffee and went to the bathroom and Stella came in as he was shaving.

She was still wearing her nightgown but she had earrings on, big silver bangles that clanked as she tilted her head from side to side and looked over his shoulder into the mirror. She saw that he was regarding her reflection and she smiled back at his image in the glass. They gazed at one another in the mirror. LaRoche had shaving cream on his cheeks and Stells had those big earrings on and their reflected faces were side by side.

"I thought I might go out to lunch, dear," she said.

"Fine."

"If you won't be coming home."

"Yes, fine."

"I was wondering . . . do you suppose these earring are too heavy for daytime?"

Stella seldom asked his opinions on matters of taste and LaRoche understood that she was being kind and sympathetic because he had to work so hard. He thought the earrings were too big.

"They're fine," he told her.

When LaRoche got to Jarvis Street, Greene was already there and waiting for him.

"The girl lived in the building," Greene said.

"Alone?"

"Apparently she lived with a man."

"Who's gone?"

"White."

"Okay," LaRoche said. That was routine. No one thought her boyfriend had killed her.

"There's another thing, Steve . . ."

LaRoche knew from the tone of Greene's voice that he wasn't going to like this.

"The guy from the Kind Edward . . . the one that talked to Billings . . . he got my message and stopped by a few minuted ago."

"You got his statement?"

"Yeah. But . . . I asked him to wait."

"Oh?"

"I think you ought to talk to him, Steve."

"Why?"

"He still insists it wasn't human."

"Oh, Jesus. Pearsall saw the sonuvabitch."

"This guy saw . . . something."

"Yeah, well . . . that's no reason to waste my time. I'd rather talk to him if he knew it was human and could give us a description, Joe. I told you."

"Ike Clanton wasn't so sure it was human. Steve, I think you want . . . don't want . . . it seems as if maybe you don't want to believe that there might be . . . something . . ."

"You bet your ass I don't."

Greene shrugged. He tossed the report on the

148

desk. LaRoche ignored it.

"What about Pearsall?" he asked.

"He said he'd be in." Greene looked at his watch. "He's a little late but . . ."

"So was I," LaRoche said.

Greene didn't know what to make of that and whether it related to Pearsall or to himself or simply objectively to the chronic fact. He paused for a moment, then said, "But I imagine that he'll come in eventually. He'd seemed all right, they said. Last night. Considering what he'd seen. He's got a record, by the way, Steve. Nothing serious."

"He didn't do it."

"No. No, he didn't. And he's not going to find a picture of the one who did, either, Steve . . ."

"Meaning what?"

"Meaning we let him look, just like we let Ike Clanton look, but he won't find anything."

LaRoche gave Greene a long look.

"You want this guy from the King Eddie to look?"

"That's not exactly . . ."

"I'll tell you what, Joe. Why don't you take him around to the dog pound? He can look at all the dogs and maybe he'll spot the killer. Hmmmm? Take an artist. Take a photographer. Draw hats and coats on pictures of the dogs. Draw neckties on them. Leave no stone unturned, Joe."

"Aw, Steve . . ."

"Don't worry about wasting time. Take all the time you need. It will be spent as usefully as going to see some guy who writes book about wolves . . ."

"Woman."

"What?"

"She's a woman, actually," Greene said. He was holding himself in, keeping a lid on his anger and frustration.

"Wonderful," LaRoche said.

"And I want to talk to you about her, too, Steve. But right now this guy is waiting here and that's his statement on your desk . . . that one you didn't seem to notice . . ."

Greene paused, thinking that maybe he had gone too far there; LaRoche did not relish sarcasm.

But LaRoche sighed and picked up the statement. He looked balefully at it. He snorted.

"What, no wings?" he said. "You mean we can eliminate hawks and vultures? Anteaters . . . we can leave them out; this guy is observant, he'd have spotted an anteater's nose straight off, I reckon."

But then LaRoche figured he was being too sarcastic, and he said, "Well, bring him in."

Greene nodded crisply and went out. He was back a moment later with the man who'd made the statement. LaRoche was still looking at it and he waited until the man was standing in front of his desk. Then he looked up. The fellow was neatly dressed and looked sober and respectable—far more so than Gary Pearsall, who was certain that the killer was a human.

LaRoche was irrationally annoyed that he did not look like a crazed drunkard. He was looking helpful, pleased with himself for doing his duty.

LaRoche handed him the statement.

"Is that what you maintain?" he asked.

He wanted the man to see how absurd it looked on paper and he wanted to judge the man's eyesight, as well. He wore glasses and faulty vision was as good an excuse as anything else. The man didn't answer for a moment. He was reading the statement, holding it far out in front of him with his eyes turning as he followed the lines. He saw them, all right; he could see. He might have been looking for spelling mistakes or grammatical errors, so carefully did he read it; he might, for crissake, have been searching for split infinitives. To carefully seek a split infinitive, LaRoche thought, and he snorted.

"Well?"

"That's about right," he said.

"About right? Or exactly right?"

Jesus, Greene thought . . . don't hedge on it now; I'll be the fool if you equivocate, fella.

"Well . . . it's right, yes."

"That's what you claim?"

"That's what I saw."

"You've had time to think about it . . . do you still say that it was an animal?"

The man glanced at the statement again, as if to see if that was, indeed, what he maintained.

"It was."

He held the statement out. LaRoche avoided taking it for a moment, his eyes gliding away as if it were a card being offered by a mute beggar. Then he took it and looked at it. The man shifted his weight from foot to foot.

"We have other witnesses," LaRoche said, slowly, thinking about it as he spoke.

"You do?" The man sounded surprised, perhaps interested. "Others have seen this . . .?"

"Other witnesses have seen the murderer," LaRoche said, cutting him off. "You are not, properly, a witness to anything. You may have seen something. No doubt you did. But if what you saw

was not a man, then it wasn't the killer." He looked up. "Thank you for stopping by."

Greene was sorry he'd insisted on bringing the
man in; the man was not ready to leave yet.

"But what was it?" he asked.

Greene said, "We'll look into it, sir."

The man half turned away, with a shrug. But he
didn't move toward the door. He looked back over
his shoulder, standing sideways. "Other witnesses .
. ." he said, thoughtfully, and he shrugged again.
Greene noticed that the had big shoulders.
LaRoche looked pained and Greene felt that
LaRoche's attitude was wrong and the man from
the King Edward just stood there, solid and stub-
born in the face of his dismissal.

"I've been thinking about this thing I saw," he
said. "I don't suppose that you believe in . . . werewolves?"

The word sprang out.

Greene actually jumped slightly.

It was a word that had been hanging unspoken
over that office and now it was out. It was almost a
relief to Greene, who could never have said it first.

"Certainly not," LaRoche said. "Do you?"

"I didn't."

"Yes. Well. We appreciate your coming forward, sir . . . with the facts as you saw them. But
you may leave the interpretation to us, if you will."

He sounded cold and scornful but the man was
not impressed. He turned back and leaned on
LaRoche's desk with both hands. He thrust his jaw
out. He had seemed a mild sort of fellow when
Greene had questioned him, earlier, but he did not
look so mild now. He was looming right over
LaRoche and he looked so belligerent that Greene

moved a step closer.

He said, "Well, now . . . that's easy enough for you to say, I guess. But you have no jurisdiction over my thoughts . . . and what I saw . . ." He grimaced. He seemed to be seeing it again, in his memory, and he reached up and took his spectacles off, as if to block out the sight.

They were thick spectacles and without them his face was cold and hard as stone.

He might have said more but LaRoche cut him off.

"Thank you, Mr. James," said LaRoche.

Chapter Forty-One

It was morning and the light from the window slid lightly across the wooden floor, as if willing to touch you tentatively upon such squalor. Paul James watched it come. He might have been watching a sun dial. He had been awake for some time but he was still lying on the mattress, smoking a cigarette and tipping the ashes into the neck of an empty beer bottle. When the light reached the mattress, he would get up, he thought. Sarah had not come home and he was thinking about that, thinking seriously and trying not to let anger and jealousy lever his ideas out of place. It wasn't easy. They were heavy thoughts and emotion kept trying to pry them up so that he could see the dark underside.

Well, it had happened before.

She would be home, in due course, not contrite but defiant, challenging him to castigate her for her ways.

Maybe, someday, she would not come home.

Maybe he would not be there, someday, when she did.

He tipped some ash on the floor. He watched the sunlight advance floorboard by floorboard. He closed his eyes for a moment, then opened them fast, as if to catch the light rushing forward to envelope him unawares. But the light had not increased its pace; you could depend on light.

The waterpipes were banging and rattling.

When the knock sounded on the door, Paul thought it was the pipes; when it sounded again, with more authority, he was surprised. He got up and pulled a bathrobe on and opened the door.

"Oh," he said.

His first thought was that he had been busted as an illegal immigrant. He wondered if his father—for his own good, certainly—had tipped them off.

There were two of them, a uniformed cop and a man in mufti. The uniformed cop had a red band around his hat, just like the Salvation Army, so that it was hard to take her seriously, but the plain-cothesman looked grim.

Paul wasn't troubled.

If they deported him he could come back soon enough . . . or not, as he chose.

"Paul James?" the uniformed cop asked.

Paul nodded. He felt weary.

"May we step in, sir?"

Paul moved aside. The uniformed cop came in first; the other followed. Paul pushed the door closed, noticing that the crack between the door and jam was getting wider. It was a relationship, like any other; things were close and things were distant. He turned, standing with his back to the lopsided door, as if he had tricked the cops into the room and wasn't going to let them out again.

One of the cops mentioned Sarah.

Sarah? Paul wondered. Had Sarah turned him in? Had she gone to the law, against all her principles?

"Miss Carlyle." It was the cop in mufti.

"She isn't here," Paul said.

"She does reside here?"

Paul nodded.

What was this? The cop in mufti was saying, "I'm afraid we have some bad news for you, Mr. James," and Paul was thinking: Why would she have done that? That wasn't the sort of thing that Sarah would do. And when they told him and Paul stared at them and they had to tell him again, because it hadn't seemed to register. He leaned back against the door. The door didn't quite fit the frame and his mind didn't quite fit his brain for a little while and he was too much out of alignment to understand and he felt nothing at all.

And there wasn't much and maybe there never had been.

They did not even ask Paul to identify the body, for they had not been married; Paul was only her roomate; her father had been sent for. Paul had never met her father and he wondered if that was significant.

They had a few questions they wanted to ask him.

He nodded, not paying much attention.

He had begun to walk around the room, here and there, the way Sarah had often paraded naked . . . but not in the winter, he thought; she had not liked being cold.

He was ignorning the cops, who were exchanging glances. Then the uniformed cop began to follow Paul around the room, in his footsteps. He had his notebook out. The detective was moving around, too, but in different directions, looking. He didn't expect to find anything there but, had there been anything he would have found it. He was White, the investigating detective from the division and he had seen Sandy Dawson's body as well as Sarah Carlyle's and he'd seen the full report on the other girl, too, although that was a different division, and he knew damn well that this kid was not the killer. He was her roommate, that was all. He noted that there was only the one mattress on the floor but that did not matter, he was not investigating sleeping arrangements.

He turned at the corner and found himself face to face with Paul, who had been pacing down the adjacent wall. It surprised them both.

Paul said, "Excuse me," just as if he had

bumped into a stranger on the street.

He was answering questions over his shoulder.

White had briefed the uniformed cop on what to ask so that he would be free to study the boy's reactions. It was the way he liked to work, holding back and not intruding. Each time the cop asked a question, he glanced at White, however, to see what marks he was getting as an interrogator. That would have ruined White's system, except that Paul did not notice. What? he said. And how? How was she killed? And where? He was in a daze. No, he didn't know where she'd been the night before . . . it wasn't unusual for her to stay out overnight, although not exactly a common occurrence . . . . she had no particular friends that he knew about . . . well, yes, she had gone out because she was annoyed, but they hadn't exactly had a fight . . . she'd been angry because he had gone to a baseball game. With his father. That was right, a baseball game. The cops looked at one another. What a reason to die. Sure, he'd heard the cop cars in the street; that was nothing rare in this neighborhood. No, he had no alibi? Did he need one? White shook his head. The cops were looking at Paul; they seemed concerned rather than suspicious. He was moving about like an automaton and answering the questions like a recording. His father had been there for awhile, but had left before Sarah was killed . . . .

The uniformed cop jumped on that one—although White rolled his eyes, seeing it clearly—and Paul didn't understand why the cop got excited.

"How do you know what time she was killed?"

"Why, no," he said. "I don't know what time

she was killed. But if it had happened before Dad left, he would have found the body on the way out, wouldn't he?"

The uniformed cop looked sheepish. White took over the questioning and the cop knew he'd been over-eager. But he was ambitious. He wanted to be promoted so that he could wear plainclothing and not have to wear that hat with the silly red band around it.

They left soon after and Paul was alone.

He was amazed to find that the sunlight had not yet reached the edge of the mattress. He waited until it did. Then he phoned his father at the King Edward.

Chapter Forty-Two

"She's interesting, Steve . . . . I think that you should have a talk with her."

"What the hell for?" LaRoche said.

"You know what for."

"I know it was no wolf; I know that."

"So does she."

"Well then?"

"There are things . . ." Greene broke off with a shrug that could easily have been extended to a shudder. He said, "You do see how the descriptions . . . vary?"

LaRoche looked balefully at him.

"We can't ignore it, Steve . . ."

"All eye witness accounts vary, Joe," LaRoche told him. "You know that. Even when two people see the same thing at the same moment, their accounts differ. In this case . . . the light was different, the shadows deeper, one man is more imaginative than the other . . . or more sober . . . more impressionable . . ."

"Yeah. But it isn't that they vary, it's how they vary. We have three different witnesses . . ."

"Two," said LaRoche. "We have Clanton and Pearsall. James saw . . . something . . . in a different place. If he did see something; if he isn't just a nut. There's no connection."

Doggedly, Greene said, "Still, he did report what he saw before the first murder was discovered . . . so we can discount the idea that he might have been inspired by a newspaper account or whatever . . ."

LaRoche nodded; he had thought of that.

"Anyhow, just suppose, for a moment, that James saw the same man that Clanton and Pearsall saw. Okay?"

LaRoche saw that Greene was determined to go on with this. He felt as if he were being lectured by some timid tutor who insisted on drumming facts into his student but feared for his job. Still, he'd said man; he hadn't used any other word. LaRoche leaned back in his chair.

Greene held three fingers up, splayed apart; his little finger was folded into his palm and his thumb held it there, like the latch on a jewel box. He said, "Pearsall says that it was a man." He pumped his hand up and down. "Clanton says it was not an animal—a subtle distinction." His hand pumped a second time. "James says it was an animal dressed like a man . . . or a man-like animal. Now, if this man . . . I say man, Steve; don't misunderstand me . . . changing . . . passing through degrees of . . ." he paused. There was a word that Cronski had taught him the night before and he wasn't sure if LaRoche would know what it meant . . . "transmogrification," he said.

LaRoche knew the word.

He knew what it meant and he knew what Greene was getting at. He said. "We'll solve this, Joe . . . with police method and, maybe guns . . . not wooden stakes and garlic."

Greene let out a deep breath.

"I'm not talking about magic, Steve. Myth, maybe. But myths are based on facts. Cronski can explain this better than I can . . ."

Greene was still holding three fingers up; now he released his little finger and it jumped up; he held his hand out, palm turned upwards.

"Not a wolf," said LaRoche.

"No," Greene whispered. "But, maybe, not quite a man . . . "

LaRoche had his fountain pen out. It occurred to Greene that he used that fountain pen the way a British officer used a swagger stick and he saw it as a weakness. LaRoche had the top off the pen and he had opened a bottle of ink. He seemed to be concentrating hard on what he was doing as he drove the sharp tip into the hear of the inkwell. He squeezed the reservoir and the ink slurped out.

But he was waiting for Greene to continue.

The man from the King Edward had spoken a word in that office and broken the ban, unlocked the syllables, so that Greene could use the other word. The other word was bigger and better; it sounded more respectable, more feasable . . .

"Lycanthropy," said Greene.

LaRoche did not react. Greene hoped that he knew what it meant, because he didn't want to have to define it. But LaRoche's expression told him nothing.

Greene said, "You know?"

"Loup garoux," said LaRoche.

Greene didn't get it.

"Werewolf," LaRoche said, with a strange smile.

"Oh," said Greene.

He was wondering if LaRoche had said it in French for the same reason that he had used the Greek root word, to make it sound more respectable an feasable and . . . possible. But no . . . LaRoche had grown up in Quebec, that was all. Still, he knew what the word meant.

"Cronski told me . . ." Greene began.

"Is she a suspect?" LaRoche asked, throwing Greene off stride.

"Why, no . . . of course not. A small woman . . ."

"But why not? If you believe in shape changing, where are the limits? Couldn't she gain fifty pounds . . . grow long hair and sharp fangs . . . and gain the terrible strength that it took to tear those girls apart?"

Greene thought that LaRoche was mocking him.

"Not shape changing," he said. That was another expression that Cronski had taught him. "A disease . . ."

"Yes. I know. Lycanthropy."

"You know about that, huh?"

"Yeah, I know," LaRoche said. "I know it's bullshit."

But then he said, "All right, Joe. Let's go see her."

Chapter Forty-Three

The rusting fire escape peeled away from the building like the backbone from a fish. It creaked and groaned and swayed. A dust of mortar drifted from the moorings. Several times Paul thought it was going to collapse as he went down, but he had to take the chance.

Paul simply could not bring himself to go down

the stairs, at the foot of which she had died. He didn't want to see the hallway and he didn't want to pass through it with his eyes closed—as Sarah had passed through his life. They had hardly touched. They had brushed together at the edges. The cops had not asked him to identify the body. They had sent for her father, instead. The summed it up, thought Paul, as he swayed on the iron rungs with dust drifting into his hair.

Paul had never met her father, who sent money from home. He supposed her father would take her body home to be buried, as well. He sent checks out and now he collected the body in return. You got what you paid for; it was the Capitalist System. He would probably collect her meager possessions, too, bundling them up neatly and keeping them in her memory. It was wrong yet strangely right that it should be so.

Paul guessed he wouldn't go to the funeral.

He was at the bottom of the fire escape and he hung there for a moment, then dropped the last few feet. His foot slipped and he banged his knee against the wall but he was pretty numb and it didn't hurt much. He rubbed it, but that was from habit, not to sooth the pain. He was in the alley. There was a ruptured and abandoned tire there, but Paul could look at that; it was not like the hallway. He walked around it and went out into the street just as Harland pulled up.

Paul got in the car.

They sat there as they had sat there in the same spot the night before, while Paul wondered if he should ask his father up for a beer; now he could think of nothing whatsoever that he might ask him.

"Paul . . . what can I say?"

"Nothing."

"I'm sorry, Paul . . ."

He gripped Paul's shoulder. Paul nodded.

"I feel as if it were my fault."

"I need a drink, Dad."

"Of course, you do. It was my fault, Paul."

"What? What are you saying?"

Harland gave him a level gaze.

"If I hadn't come here . . . annoyed your girl . . ."

"It wasn't that. She might have gone out, anyhow. Let's not talk about it, okay?"

Harland nodded but he did not start the car.

Paul said, "She was killed in the hallway . . ."

"You told me. On the phone."

"I came down the fire escape."

"I understand . . ."

"No, you don't. They sent for her father to identify the body and I came down the fire escape. I don't want to go back to that apartment."

"Why, I guess you wouldn't. You can't live here, now . . . you can't go in and out of that building as if . . . well, you can stay with me, Paul. At the hotel. Until you decide what you want to do now; where you want to go . . ."

"Don't . . . don't make any suggestions, okay?"

"Why, no."

"Let's go, okay?"

Harland touched the ignition key but did not turn it.

He said, "If you're not coming back here, Paul, maybe I ought to go up and fetch your things?"

"No!"

"I'll do it; you won't have to go in."

"I don't want them. Sarah's father will collect her things. I was thinking about that."

"Well, of course he will."

"I don't want anything from that apartment . . . that life."

Harland couldn't seem to comprehend that.

"Your clothing," he said. "I saw that you had quite a few books there . . ."

"Jesus," said Paul.

"Oh. Well . . ."

"Material possessions, Dad," Paul said. "Oh, how Sarah ranted and raved about material possessions. A person was owned by their possessions, she said. Yet she liked nice things; she bought a new dress with money from home. Then she spilled wine on it. The stain never did come out. Maybe she did it deliberately, I don't know. She wouldn't have known herself. She had ideals but they didn't fit quite right in her head, they were just stuffed in their every which way with the edges rubbing together. Lots of friction, when the edge on an idea starts rubbing against a concept. Enough friction to start a fire . . . chock-a-block full of ideas that didn't fit. Big, solid blocks of conviction, slices of platitude, lumps of dedication shouldered out of position by wedges of habit . . . all cluttered up, Dad . . ."

Harland was staring at his son, just as the policemen had, with concern. He patted his shoulder. He turned the key and the engine caught and he patted Paul's shoulder again.

"I guess maybe you're in sort of shock," he said.

He doesn't understand, thought Paul.

"We won't worry about your things for now,"

Harland said.

"Jesus! Can't you see . . .?"

"Why, I guess I can, Paul . . ."

Then Harland astounded Paul.

"You're going to leave your things behind as a tribute to Sarah," he said.

"Why . . . that's right!"

And it was. His father amazed him.

Chapter Forty-Four

Lips drawn back from gleaming fangs, the big timber wolf was motionless yet seemed ready to move instantly, to snap or spring, its taut body vibrant with static energy.

The woman crawled towards the wolf.

She had a dead rabbit in her hands. The rabbit's neck was broken, its head flopped back and forth. She crawled right up to the wolf. The wolf's eyes were yellow; its fangs were white. The woman put the rabbit down in the grass before the wolf and sat back on her heels, almost as if she were kneeling in homage before the beast.

Then she leaned back further, tilting her head, to see if the arrangement was satisfactory.

She was doing that when LaRoche and Greene came around the barricade that closed off this unfinished panorama.

LaRoche was looking sour.

He had just found out that you had to pay to get into the museum; he'd always thought that museums were free—and knew damned well that they should be.

Cronski heard them coming.

She rose and stepped down from the platform, automatically brushing at her knees, although the grass and dirt was plastic and had not soiled her slacks. Greene had phoned her earler and they'd agreed to meet here. Greene thought it a singularly appropriate place to talk, with the wolves grouped around them. It was better than the zoo. The stuffed wolves waited with infinite patience for your leisurely inspection.

"Sergeant Greene," Cronski said.

Greene had not decided how to address his strange woman. He said, "Ma'am" and felt like a cowboy.

He introduced her to LaRoche.

"Do you like the panorama?" she asked. "It's not quite finished. I wanted to apply the final touches myself; one gets a feeling for the little details. The big fellow in the foreground has just killed the rabbit, you see; he's looking up to make sure he has no competition for the kill."

The two cops looked at the panorama, dutifully

showing an interest.

Then LaRoche said, "I've always been sort of fond of wolves, myself."

He obviously meant it. Cronski smiled.

Then he said. "About this other stuff . . ."

Greene frowned. LaRoche knew the word. Why had he said *stuff*? Why did he act less informed and more skeptical than he was? Did he have a reason, or was it just his way? He hoped LaRoche was not going to embarrass him.

LaRoche said, "I'll listen."

Cronski said, "But what will you listen to?"

"Well, I'm not going to question you."

Greene put in, "If you could just tell him what you told me, please . . . about how the legend got started, where myth and reality meet . . ."

" . . . in a shadowy transition," she said, finishing the sentence that Greene was quoting from her. She was smiling. Greene figured that, no matter how LaRoche behaved, he would not be able to embarrass this woman; at the most, she would be tolerantly amused by him.

Cronski sat on the edge of the platform. LaRoche put one foot up and rested his hands on his raised knee.

"I don't believe in werewolves," said Cronski.

"Nobody does," LaRoche said.

He grinned.

"But plenty of people are scared of them, even if they don't believe in them."

"Oh, my, yes," she agreed.

Greene decided this meeting was going to go okay.

LaRoche said, "It wouldn't be so good if people got the idea that these murders were committed by something . . . other than a man. A wolf . . . or . . . whatever . . ."

"Yes. It must not be blamed on an innocent wolf."

"We agree," LaRoche said.

"As for the other . . ."

"Tell me," said LaRoche.

"Yes. I said that I don't believe in werewolves. I meant, in the proper sense, of course. Let me make that clear. I don't believe that a man can take the shape of a wolf . . . can make a full transition. However . . . a wolfman; that is a different matter. And it is the wolfman that our society has been conditioned to think of, when they consider the werewolf. Hollywood has shaped out thoughts here and we think of a werewolf as looking like Lon Chaney, rather than like a wolf. In this instance, Hollywood is probably closer to the truth than are the legends. And I . . . I believe such things can be . . . and are . . ."

LaRoche shifted his foot an inch; he didn't look skeptical. He didn't look fascinated, either, as Greene was—he just looked patient, like the waiting wolves.

Cronski said, "The belief in werewolves predates Christianity and was far more common before the Christian era, in fact; in Christian times, instances of lycanthropy were often confused with possession by the devil. I don't believe in the devil," she added, smiling. "Werewolves are far more interesting. And plausible. Well. The belief is ancient. It is also so widespread throughout the world that it seems it must have begun in the very dawn of time . . . when men were not, perhaps, so very different from the beasts. These things must have oc-

-curred frequently and ubiquitously. Lykon is the first of which we know; I doubt he was really the first. Nor is it always the poor wolf that gets the blame. In South America, there are jaguar men. In Africa, there are leopard men and crocodile men.

"There was Nebuchadnezzar," said LaRoche, grinning.

"What?" said Greene, surprised.

But Cronski laughed.

"Ah, yes . . . the boanthrope," she said. "You are not, I think, as skeptical as you appear . . ."

"Well, I don't believe in bull men," said LaRoche. He didn't say bullshit, but he implied it.

"Nebuchadnezzar believed himself an ox," Cronski told Greene, who was looking bemused.

How in hell did LaRoche know that? he wondered.

Cronski said, "Well, the animal varies from place to place, and time to time, but the legend is much the same. A man becomes the animal most feared in the area. The wolf was the largest predator in Northern Europe . . . thus we have the wolfman. But it was a poor choice, the wolf; a regrettable choice. The wolf is a social animal, dependent on the pack, with instincts of loyalty . . . whereas the wolfman is by nature and necessity apart and alone. However, it is not the nature of the wolf that matters; rather it is the nature that the wolfman believes the wolf to have. The mind creates the pattern and makes it reality. I believe that has happened and does happen; not so often now as in times gone by, when such things were not considered impossible and men were not quite men. Primordial man knew himself as a part of nature; he did not distinguish between human and

170

animal—nor burden himself with the concept of a soul. Well, that is irrelevant; we are talking of now. A man believes himself a beast . . . and becomes a beast . . .''

"In his mind," LaRoche said.

"Oh, he changes. It is in his mind that the change is effected, but his body changes."

LaRoche frowned. "You said . . ."

"They change. They do not change into wolves, but they are no longer men. A man afflicted by this . . . disorder . . . looks at the full moon . . . and is no longer a man."

"How do they change? In what way?"

"The mind changes. And the mind shapes the body."

"Do you mean this literally? Physically?"

"Oh, yes. Quite. What is more malleable than flesh? The body is in a state of change through all its time. We grow big, we grow old, we die and corrupt . . . it is the same body, it has changed. You do not look now as you did last year, Sergeant LaRoche. Nor as you looked as a child. And what is the body, at that? No more than a corpse supported by the spirit . . . by the mind . . . by the soul, if you will. So why should you doubt that the mind can shape the body at a whim? Indian fakirs can control the flow of blood through their veins and walk on glowing coals with flesh unaffected . . . cannot man shift the bones of his face, draw back the gums from his teeth, expel his beard? It seems not so unlikely."

LaRoche started to speak, then hesitated; he frowned, more with concentration than with doubt.

"You do not believe this?" Cronski said.

"No . . ." he said, slowly.

"But you are locked within the modern concept of time . . . as is the wolfman himself, which makes him far more rare today than in an age when mankind shared the same chronic senses as the beasts. The wolfman, as a man, cannot believe that he can change . . . and makes it less likely."

LaRoche shifted his weight and said, "What does our sense of time have to do with it?"

Cronski turned her face, as if she were looking for time itself, to point it out to him.

"You have seen dead men," she said.

LaRoche nodded.

"You have seen men alive and then you have seen them dead. The body decays, the flesh becomes putrid. Yet it is the same body. You accept the change because time has passed. You will accept the fact that your children will grow year by year . . . but you would go mad if a child suddenly aged before your eyes. Yet why not? Why should it not be? Time does not bow to our wishes, nor suspend itself to our commands. Time laughs at Einstein. And yet, perhaps, to the instictive, primordial command of the wolfman . . ."

She shrugged.

"I should like to see it happen," she said.

"I wouldn't," said Joe Greene, and he shivered. They did not speak for awhile.

They all looked at the panorama and it was static; the wolves were stuffed and did not change at all.

LaRoche spoke first. "I don't believe it," he said. "I think you do. If it were possible . . . if such a thing could be . . . how do we find a wolfman? Can you tell me that? Would his actions be predictable? Would he lead a normal life, as a man, when he was not changed? When he did not think of himself as a wolf? Would he remember the things he did in his other form? Are there certain places he would go? Would he have a conscience?"

LaRoche had rattled the questions off in fast order. Greene was amazed to realize that LaRoche must have thought of them before. LaRoche was always surprising him.

Then LaRoche was smiling.

"And when we find him," he said. "Will we need a silver bullet?"

"The legend predates bullets," said Cronski.

She thought about it.

"And silver, too," she said.

She thought some more.

"I do not know," she said.

She had taken the question seriously and again they did not speak for awhile.

"But you did not come here to listen to my theories," Cronski said. "You wish me to help you find this . . . killer. It may be that I can. Whether the change is real, or simply in his mind, perhaps I can advise you. But your questions . . . I can't answer them; I do not know the answers. I wish I did. Once, not so long ago, a man came to me . . ."

She broke off, as if deciding that she would not tell them about that. She began again.

"Once, in the mountains of northern Greece, I think that I saw a wolfman. I can not swear to it. I saw . . . something. I was on a motoring holiday; I had stopped beside the road in a desolate wilderness . . . at night. I heard it, first, and then I saw it. It moved through stunted trees, under a full moon. It looked at me; I looked at it. Its eyes were burning like hot sulphur, yellow eyes; its teeth were white as bones and it was hunting. But I was not afraid of it, for I was fascinated. There are worse ways to die than that . . . the fang and claw are natural and nothing is more natural than death dealt by the predator to its prey. But it did not attack me . . . because I had no fear. It senses this, and knew I was not the natural prey of its bloodlust. Had I showed fear, had I fled . . . but I did not. It moved off. I could hear it breathing long after I could no longer see it. Then I was afraid, for it was awesome. I returned to my motorcar and went on to the nearest village. In the tavern, I told them what I had seen. My Greek is not good, but they knew the word, lycanthropy, once I emphasized the right syllable. The men laughed. They were handsome men, and happy. They danced and bought me wine and they drank and, tilting their faces to the full moon, they howled with glee. But the women saw no fun in this and looked nervous, with their worry beads in their hands and their black shawls drawn tight across their fluttering throats . . ."

Cronski paused and her eyes came back into focus.

"Perhaps I saw only a hermit," she said, with a sigh.

Greene felt the hairs rise along his neck. Could a man expel his hairs? He believed her—and believed it was no hermit she had seen in the wilderness.

LaRoche waited a moment. It was impossible to tell how mcuh her tale had affected him. Then he said, "You started to say something else . . . about a man who came to you not long ago . . ." With his policeman's mind, he had been jarred by the abrupt way she had cut them off and veered from it.

"Yes," she said. "But that . . . he thought . . . he came to me as a man and told me a thing . . . but he was a man; perhaps he was mistaken, or a liar."

Of that she would say no more.

But she said, "A motive."

And when LaRoche raised his eyebrows, she said, "I think you will find that he has a motive, a reason to kill or a justification for killing. That is the help I can offer you, the advice, for what it is worth."

"I don't understand that," said LaRoche. "If it were true, if this killer were a wolfman, or thought he was . . . wouldn't blood lust be reason enough? Wouldn't his belief that he must kill be motive enough?"

"At one time, it was enough, and more," Cronski said. "But just as man no longer shares the animal's sense of time, so does he require more than a simple desire to kill. We live in a world of morality and sin and the feeble justifications thereof, you see. Man excuses his sins and rationalizes his crimes and confesses his guilt, seeking absolution. A modern man is not the same as primitive man, content to act on impulse; he must have reasons. His mind requires motivation. And a wolfman . . . is still a man—when he is not a wolf. His mind will not effect the change without justification, nor will he change—and kill—merely by the cycle of the moon. But this man, with the power to change already in his blood, given a reason to kill—then will be become a wolfman, and kill as a beast."

LaRoche licked his lips. They were dry. He said, "Is that a theory or do you have some reason to believe it true?"

"Oh reasons . . . what are reasons? Do I require reasons, just as the wolfman does?"

She stood up and gazed into the panorama.

She seemed suddenly perturbed, as if she might have said more than she wished to—as if she hadn't intended to help or, perhaps, had betrayed a trust.

LaRoche said, "I can't see how there can be a reason for these murders. The three girls were not connected in any way. Unless the simple fact that they were young and pretty and alone . . . unless that is a motive . . ."

"Well, it's nothing to me," she said. "You will have to do the police work; I've said all I can."

"Well, thank you," LaRoche said.

Expert at dismissing men from his office, he knew she had dismissed them from her panorama.

"Of course," she said.

She turned away. LaRoche took his foot from the platform and nodded to Greene. They started to move off. But the Cronski turned to them again.

"If you do find him . . ." she said.

"Yes?"

"You will be afraid. You are not me; you will show your fear and he will . . . well, you must be careful. Of the silver bullet, I can't say; that may be nonsense or . . . it may be founded on some fact unknown to me. But . . . he will be very, very strong; he will be fast and savage. He will be superhuman and unlike anything you have met before. These are qualities that the mind can lend the body, beyond the normal boundaries of man. And you will show your fear . . ."

Greene felt icy cold; he was already frightened.

"And you will have to kill him," she said. "You know that? You will not take him captive."

"I know that," said LaRoche. "If it were true."

"He will take far more killing than would a man," she said. "Far, far more . . . for the mind has no bones to break and the mind can make a dead man walk . . ."

Chapter Forty-Five

She had told them that they would have to kill him and she knew that was true but she regretted it. To study such a man, to learn the ways of his dark powers, actually to be present when he changed—N.V. Cronski would have gladly given her life for such an opportunity.

But it would not be, she thought, sadly.

It could not be and it was that knowledge that disturbed her and changed her mood so that she had dismissed the policemen so abruptly. It was a shame that those young girls had been killed, of course; she knew that she should regret that . . . but what was death to knowledge? Death was the most natural thing of all, far more natural than life, for life is ephemeral, even accidental—and death is eternal.

And he would have to die.

She sat there on the rim of the wolf pack and thought about such things.

If the police found him transmogrified, they would have to kill him—if they could—for no man could subdue him or handcuff him or tame him; if they deduced who he was and captured him as a man, then they could take him alive . . . but their prisoner would be a man no more—in captivity, he would not change. The change to study him would be lost, buried in some dark cell, locked in some dungeon by those who thought only of his crimes and did not even believe that there was something more. It depressed her and filled her with bleak despair.

For N.V. Cronski was certain that it was no man who had killed those girls. She had no true reason for that conviction, nor did she need one. She sensed it.

She had seen one man with the change upon him—that time in the mountains of northern Greece—and she had met one, face to face, but he had come to her as a man and that meeting had left them both dissastified. He had come to her for help and advice, desperate to find out what he had become, and she had been more interested in what he was then in helping him. At cross purposes, they had talked, and she had no doubt whatsoever that what he told her was true. When had that been? Not so very long ago. He'd faced her across her desk and told her that he's always known that some dark power was within him, had often felt the physical pull of the moon dragging at his flesh and shifting the pattern of his bones, had often spent the long nights looking at the full moon and trembling under its gravity, feeling that something was trying to happen, was lurking just beyond fulfillment. He had read her book, among many, and had come to her as he might have gone to a priest, for absolution, rather than a scientist with whom, together, they might learn these mysteries. He sought exorcism; she sought knowledge.

As he spoke of it, she fancied she could see his face slipping out of focus, a prelude to the change—but her own eyes had been blurred by excitement.

And he had not changed.

He had only changed once. He begged her to believe that, as if it were a sin, while she wished with all her heart that he would change again, before her eyes.

If he had killed her there, it would have been a small price to pay. She had tried to excite him, to anger him, to enrage him, all to no effect. He had changed but once, and there had been a reason. She must believe that, he had said, again and again; she must believe he was justified. His wife had done something—something that could not be justified—and it had justified him. He would not speak of the details, he hung his head in shame and pleaded with her for assurance that it would not happen again—even as she willed it to happen.

"I cannot say," she had told him.

"Will it happen again?" he'd asked, a pitiful creature, as a man, cringing in the shadow of his own power.

He'd grimaced. He'd rolled his eyes and gnashed his teeth and clenched his fists.

But he had remained a man.

"I cannot say," she told him again. "But if it does . . . come to me."

And he had not come again.

Chapter Forty-Six

Leaving the museum, neither man spoke until they were in the car. Greene was behind the wheel.

He said, "What did you think of her, Steve?"

"An unusual woman."

"Well, sure . . . but . . ." Greene was flummoxed by that understatement; then he wondered if that might be just what LaRoche intended. He could never tell about LaRoche. He said, "What did you think about . . . what she said?"

"No."

"No what?"

"I don't believe it. It's nonsense. There may be men who think themselves wolves, granted. A psychological thing, an obsession or a delusion. And they may even look unnatural . . . but naturally unnatural, if you follow me. Eyes narrowed, mouth drawn into a rictus, panting heavily . . . Well, I'll believe that; no more. No changes, Joe."

Greene put the keys in the ignition but he did not start he car yet.

"She does have a way of making it sound possible," he said. "I'm sure she believes it herself."

"She does, at that. Standing there . . . I almost believed it, myself, standing there with the wolves behind us . . ."

"You had questions for her. Steve . . . they weren't off the top of your head, you'd thought about them."

LaRoche grunted. Greene started the motor.

LaRoche said, "You know . . . I got the impression that she would like to be a werewolf herself."

"So did I."

"Imagine wanting to be a werewolf!"

"It would sell plenty of books," Greene said, sounding more cynical than he intended. "It would sure make her the world's foremost authority." He felt like laughing. He had no idea why and it was ridiculous. There were three young girls dead and there was nothing to laugh about. Maybe it was just because he was out of the museum; you couldn't laugh inside a museum. He said, "I guess you figure that it was a waste of time, going to see her, huh?"

"I don't know. Maybe not. What I told her at

the beginning, Joe . . . about people being scared of werewolves . . . that's true. People are plenty scared of werewolves . . ."

Greene put the car in gear but kept his foot on the brake pedal. He sensed that LaRoche was talking around something that he couldn't say plainly.

And suddenly LaRoche was laughing.

Greene was startled. Then he was laughing, too. All of the tension of the last two days seemed to have snapped and they laughed together joyfully.

LaRoche said, "Vampires!" and he snorted.

Greene roared with good humour.

"Vampires don't scare nobody," LaRoche said. "They're too skinny! They're too pale! Vampires are sort of sexy but they don't scare nobody 'casue they are . . . get this! 'Cause they are too skinny!"

Greene was laughing so hard that he had to take the car out of gear. He leaned over the wheel, convulsed by great racking bursts of laughter. He had never heard anything so funny.

"Frankenstein!" he shouted.

"Don't scare a soul," LaRoche said. "He's too fat!"

"He's got club feet!" Greene squealed. "He's got a square head! He can't scare nobody!"

"He's got . . ." LaRoche doubled over, laughing as hard as a man could laugh . . . "He's got pins in his neck!"

And they laughed together, sitting in the car, and after awhile they took turns laughing, with the tears streaming down their faces. One would stop and the other would begin and the laughter communicated itself back and forth like the plague.

Then they stopped laughing.

Greene blew his nose.

"But people are scared of werewolves, though," LaRoche said, and it wasn't funny this time. "So let's nobody mention werewolves, Joe . . ."

Chapter Forty-Seven

And people were scared and werewolves were mentioned.

There had been three grotesque deaths under the full moon and the newspapers sounded the tones of sensationalism. Even the negatives were sensational as headlines cried: DEAD GIRLS NOT DEVOURED and WOLF NOT REPONSIBLE FOR GORY DEATHES. Art Rose and his like spread a smorgasbord of morbid speculation across the columns; gruesome details were stacked one upon the other, just like the newspapers themselves, awaiting delivery; the hungry public gorged on this feast.

And when three days went by without another murder, it was mentioned that the moon was gibbous.

No further victims were found. That did not mean that there were none. The Drummond girl had been discovered by the chance bounce of a baseball and Toronto was a town filled with homeless young runaway girls . . . already reported missing, they might now be dead. The police looked for things they did not want to find, and they looked for the man they wanted very much to find. Police patrols were out in force and decoys, both women and men dressed as women, wandered into dark and deserted places, looking as young and helpless as they could.

A steady line of joggers clumped down Scholar's Walk, past the patrol car parked on the grass. They followed so close upon one another that they might have been coupled like railroad cars, at the hips. In the car, Silvia and Sutton, in uniform but with their hats off, watched the joggers. The joggers all had the same expression, deliberate, concentrating, a bit smug because they were getting fashionable fit. Silvia and Sutton both had the same expression, as well. They looked sour. They could almost hear the jogger's backbones jarring out of place and just knew they were knocking ten years off their lives as they followed the trend.

Silvia said, "It's a problem."

"How's that?" Sutton asked.

"Joggers. A problem. I never thought of it before. But how in hell are we supposed to tell a jogger from a fleeing fugitive? I mean, some guy snatches a handbag, he's got the Adidas running shoes, he's got the shorts, we see him running . . . how do we know he ain't a thief?"

"Ought to make jogging a crime," said Sutton, a bitter man. "Arrest all the fuckers."

Silvia nodded agreement.

"They used to call this Scholar's Walk," he said. "Now it's Asshole Run."

They nodded gravely to one another, equally distraught that pedantic contemplation had yielded to the lemming impulse.

Silvia, who was dedicated as well as disgruntled by nature, said, "What in hell are we doing here, anyhow? The killer ain't no jogger. Might be a werewolf, but he ain't no jogger."

"Oh, jeez . . . don't say things like that . . . "

"Papers said it. Cops, we ain't allowed to say what we think; ain't right."

"You don't really think that, do you?"

"Hell, no. Ain't no such thing as werewolves. It's just that I ought to have a right to say it."

"Maybe," said Silvia, doubtfully.

Then he grinned and said, "Here comes a werewolf now . . ."

They watched a big, black man come down the path, running hard. He was overtaking all the joggers and he wore a heavy sweatsuit. He was snorting but he wasn't breathing hard. This was no garden variety jogger and the cops looked at him with respect. It was Wash McCoy who, although retired from the ring, liked to keep in fighting trim, but the cops didn't know this. They did see that he was a far different proposition from the joggers, however, and it was only because he felt a patriotic need to prove that Canadians were every bit as prejudiced as Americans that Sutton said, "Look at

185

the big buck nigger run!"

In the lobby of the King Edward Hotel, two prostitutes were eyeing the trade. They felt a bit out of place in the luxury hotel, being streetwalkers by nature, but they had been frightened off the streets by the murders. They were both young. One was blonde and one had dark hair but they were equally depraved.

The saw Harland James come out of the elevator and walk across the lobby to the tobacconist.

"He must be a punter, you think?" said June.

"Looks like a punter," said Valerie, the blonde.

They drifted out to intercept him, a bit nervous with a thick carpet under their feet instead of cobblestones.

Harland came back towards the elevators.

"Looking for a good time, mister?" June asked.

He looked startled.

"I'm sorry . . . I don't . . ."

"We're hookers," June snorted, never a girl to beat around the bush.

"Oh," he said. He grinned but he was obviously embarrassed. He said, "I'm sorry . . . my son is staying with me."

He backef off and went around them, nodding sheepishly.

The girls shrugged.

They seemed to have trouble getting a proper purchase on the carpet and they were having little success working the lobby and they were deeply resentful that the murders had scared them in from the streets and alleys where, solidly fixed on concrete, they felt confident and invulnerable.

June summed it up.

"I had some kinky tricks in my life," she said.

186

"But I ain't never had no werewolf and I ain't about to . . ."

Ken Hubble was cruising, looking for women, and when he saw the tall blonde switching her ass down Spadina Avenue, he thought, This can't be bad.

He pulled the car to the curb and rolled the window down.

The blonde slowed down.

"Hey, Sweet Thing," Ken called out and, sure enough, the blonde came right over to the car.

"Want a ride?" he asked.

She gazed at him speculatively, no doubt wondering how good he was in bed, he figured; then she nodded. Ken's horny heart was filled with joy. He opened the door and she slid in. She was a big girl, but trim enough. Ken was a man who put his cards on the table and before he started the drive, he said, "I never pay for it, baby." She merely nodded. Oh boy! thought Ken. He figured to waste no time and he drove directly down to a deserted spot under the elevated highway. He parked up against the pilings, so that she was unable to open the door on her side of the car—not that he thought she would want to. She had a funny smile, as if she were forcing it. Probably nervous, he thought; maybe she never did a thing like this before but he had been unable to resist his charm.

He put his arm around her.

Christ, she felt hard as a rock . . . really tensed up. But she didn't try to push his hand away.

"What's your name, Honey?"

"Donna," she said. She had a husky voice.

Ken began to stroke her thigh.

"Stop that," she said.

She was trembling. Ken knew she must be hot as a pistol, to tremble that way, and figured she was protesting a bit so he wouldn't think that she was a tramp.

He pushed his hand right up her leg.

He looked puzzled.

Then he looked sick.

Then he was looking at a pair of handcuffs and the blonde, whose name was Donald Earl Trumbell, and who was heartily ashamed of being pretty enough to be assigned to the drag patrol, called Ken a filthy pervert as he arrested him.

Ken Hubble was released without being charged and Trumbell was castigated for jumping the gun. He had not been on the street to arrest a would-be Romeo. Other suspects were brought in, questioned and released. No one really thought they might be guilty, it was just that, in their frustration, the police felt they should do something. And there was a terrible paradox involved: If the killer did not strike again, it was doubtful that they would find them. They had two vague descriptions and one too bizarre to be seriously considered . . . and they had one fact about which they were keeping quiet, because they didn't know what it meant. There had been the saliva of a wolf. It had to mean something . . . .

In the White Rose Tavern, they talked of the murders as they talked of sports and war. Gus threw opinions out like rubber balls, bouncing them off customers. Wash McCoy was there. Wash was in meat packing; he knew how gory a dead thing could be. Ike Clanton was there. He had seen the killer and was drinking out on it. The mailman was there. He had delivered letters to one of the dead girls.

And Harland and Paul James sat there, drinking beer, and they told no one that Paul's girl had been one of the victims—or anything else.

Now that Sarah was dead, Paul had no idea what he would do with his life. Harland didn't press him. Paul was devoid of energy and initiative, willing to be led or driven. He was staying at the King Edward with Harland and they were just letting time pass. Now they were sitting at the bar and Paul drank like an automaton, like one of those little dolls that mix cocktails and quaff them down on the shelf behind the bar. His hand went up; he drank; it went down. He no longer shrugged a lot, but he stared. Harland was worried about the boy. When Paul's glass was empty, Gus filled it; Harland paid. Sometimes, in the intervals, Paul raised the empty glass and did not seem to notice the difference. It was impossible to tell if he was thinking, or what he was thinking about.

Harland had not told Paul that he had been to the police with a description of the possible killer.

What was the point of that?

"The point is," said Gus, not for the first time, "how do the parents feel? They buy a newspaper, they're trying to forget what happened, they want to maybe read the sport's page or look at the com-

189

ics, they get this newspaper and they got to read that their daughter wasn't devoured. I mean, how is that supposed to make them feel?''

"Upside down, too," the mailman said. "They got to read how she was found upside down on the stairs . . . same stairs I been up, with mail.''

"I'd like to run into this guy," Wash said, rolling his big shoulders.

"Happen you wouldn't," Ike mumbled.

Wash looked out from the tops of his eyes and said, "I got nothing in particular against murderers . . . I've known a few, myself, there were mostly okay. But a guy that wants to tear up young girls that way, a guy like that, well . . . I'd like to run into him, is all.''

"Not if you'd seen him," said Ike.

"I've heard that maybe it wasn't a guy," Gus said. "Heard talk it was something else . . .''

"How's that?"

"Just talk. Werewolf.''

Gus wiped at the surface of the bar. Harland glanced at Paul, but Paul didn't seem to have heard. Paul lifted his glass and drank; he lowered it. It was just as well that he didn't hear talk like that, Harland thought.

Wash said, "Naw. That's just in the movies.''

"That's what I told 'em," Ike said. He was wheeled up to the bar and only his eyes showed over the rim.

"I guess," said Gus.

"Like in the movies.''

"Here, Ike! You saw this guy, right? You think it could of been a werewolf?''

"How should I know? I never saw one of them. Unless that was one.''

"He have long ears? Anything like that?"

"Naw. Had a hat."

"Ain't nothing to say a werewolf can't have a hat, though. Might wear a hat to hide his ears. You think?"

Ike shrugged. He looped an arm like a derrick up to the bar with his empty glass.

Wash was considering this conversation.

He said, "How can a guy be a werewolf? Huh? I mean, a guy can drink or take dope or beat up on his old lady, sure . . . but how can a guy be a werewolf?" He snorted.

"I guess," said Gus. "You reckon?"

Ike was his usual self. He said, "The fellas I feel sorry for are the rapists."

They looked at him. Gus could only look at this forehead from behind the bar but Wash could see all there was of him. Ike didn't explain. Gus filled his glass.

"How so?" Gus asked.

Ike said, "You take your average rapist. He ain't never hurt nobody, just raped 'em, right? What's he got to think now? He can't ply his trade, he's afraid to rape somebody, 'cause if they catch him they'll think he's a werewolf. Gives a rapist a bad name."

Ike keplt a straight face. Who could tell if he meant what he said?

Harland glanced at his son again, but Paul was unaffected by the talk around him.

Harland was often that way himself. He knew the mood. After his wife had vanished, he had spent a long time being like that. Perhaps it was hereditary. Harland often wondered what was hereditary and what wasn't. It was an interesting speculation; it was something he would have liked to know. Now he looked at his son and Paul just sat there, as pliable as putty. Harland felt that if he bent the boy's arms into a new position, they would just stay there, retaining whatever shape they had been bent to.

Soon Harland would ask his son to come home.

Chapter Forty-Eight

LaRoche was furious with the newspapers and Greene couldn't blame him. They had enough to think about without worrying about public relations. The Superintendent had just phoned to suggest that LaRoche have dinner with him and they knew damned well what that meant. Suggest—hah! LaRoche was not looking forward to that. The fact that he—and his wife—had been invited to the Superintendent's own home didn't make it better; it just meant that it would be informal and that the discussion would go beyond his line-of-work duties. The politicians were getting worried, he thought; they don't want any more voters killed. Still . . . the Superintendent was probably getting plenty of pressure himself and was just passing it on. There had been those damned newspapers first; they had really stirred things up. If they ever got hold of the saliva thing . . . Lord! What could they do with that! Things were frantic enough as it was. A wizened old trapper had come in and offered to lay a line of wolf tracks down Yonge Street. Apparently he had been serious. A Texan had been turned back at the border when he showed up wearing a sixgun and announcing that he'd come to get the sonuvabitch that had been guttin' gals. That had made the papers. The sporting goods stores were doing a rare business in hunting rifles and it was rumoured that vigilante committees were being formed; they went to the pubs and talked of how they would get it, man or beast, they didn't care which; they got drunk and went home. No harm was done. But there was a thing called public relations and now LaRoche had to dine with the Superintendent and he was furious.

How could public relations take precedence over lives?

But they hadn't caught the killer and they were being made to feel humiliated and ineffective, that was the thing. What would be next? Greene wondered. Probably some disgruntled male chauvinist would demand equal rights to be murdered. That would be reported, you could bet on that. And the killer would probably chuckle when he read it. Madmen loved to read about their crimes, Greene knew; it incited them to bigger and better crimes as they sought increased press coverage. And the reporters cried about freedom of the press . . . and Steve LaRoche had to discuss it with the Superintendent . . . .

LaRoche phoned home.

He held the telephone against his ear by cradling it in his raised shoulder and while he waited for his wife to answer he whacked his fountain pen against his blotter, keeping pace, one whack for each ring.

Then she answered.

LaRoche told her they would be having dinner at the Superintendent's home.

"Oh, how wonderful!" Stella cried.

"It isn't exactly social," he said.

"How positively delightful, darling. It must be quite a feather in your cap!"

"Not exactly."

"What shall I wear?"

LaRoche tight-lipped so that he might have been either grim or fighting a smile, said, "I think I'll divorce you, Stella."

And Stella said, "The green dress, I think . . ."

LaRoche had left and Greene sat at his desk and wondered if they were doing all they could. They were patrolling in force and, in a case like this, what else could you do but wait and hope? Well. . .you could think about it. They had three different descriptions of the killer. . .two, LaRoche still maintained, but Greene felt sure it was three. If they caught him, he could be identified. Okay, that was something. The saliva. . .well, they weren't really worried about that as much as they were about keeping it out of the papers. The pathologist was running further tests on it and might turn up something, but it

194

could be explained logically enough—if the killer had access to the saliva of a wolf and was using it to confuse the issue. . .yes, that was no problem, as long as the newspapers didn't get hold of it and create even more panic. So it was a madman, killing without motive or reason, with no known connection between his victims. Or was there? All three girls had been young, unmarried and attractive, but that meant nothing other than that they were more available to the killer than housewives. They were all over the place, those young girls. So there was no motive and no connection and the killer was cunning enough to try to blame it on a wolf. . .but Greene had been skirting it and he knew it; now he had to remember what Cronski had told them—there had to be an explanation. If she were right, then there was some link, if only they could find it and recognize it.

No, that was nonsense.

It was a man—a madman, but a man—and he was just wasting his time following any other track. Still, it was hard to shake the nagging feeling that he had overlooked something.

Greene wished he could be as objective as LaRoche.

Chapter Forty-Nine

Manny Goldman was nervous when LaRoche walked into his jewelry shop on Sherbourne. He knew who LaRoche was. Manny was a fence who melted down stolen jewelry, reset it, and sold it. In lighter moments he liked to think of himself as a purloiner of fine objects. But this was not a light moment and his Adam's apple was shifting around as he smiled at the cop across the counter.

He said, "I'm clean, Sergeant. . .been clean since the last little trouble I had."

"I doubt that. . ."

"I swear. . ."

"But that's not why I'm here. I want you to do something for me."

Manny was already shaking his head.

"I won't squeal on nobody," he protested. "Anyhow, I don't know anybody to squeal on these days. I don't know nothing. I'm clean as a bleached bone."

"No, this is something else. Personal."

"Oh, well. . ." Manny said, glad to be of service.

Then LaRoche told him what he wanted and Manny was amazed. He had never thought LaRoche was the sort of man who went in for knickknacks or whatever. But he was glad to do it. It was easy enough to do and it never hurt to do a cop a favor. . . .

Chapter Fifty

Paul James was stretched out on the bed in his father's room at the King Edward. He lay as he'd gone down, one forearm across his forehead, one foot trailing over the edge of the mattress. Just like putty, Harland thought. You could twist him and shape him as you liked. Well, it must have been a terrible shock for the boy, having his girl murdered. Harland hadn't realized how greatly that would affect him. Paul hadn't been like putty at first, not at all. He'd been like a lump of ice. Maybe an iceberg, most of it submerged; maybe like that. But now he was like putty.

Harland figured that that insolent, depraved girl had used him like putty, too; she had shaped him to her purposes and come close to ruining his life. Well, that was over. Harland felt responsible for Paul, because he was his father, of course, and because maybe he had passed that pliable trait on to the boy. Paul's mother had always been able to shape and mold Harland, too, bending him and twisting him into awful configurations and terrible designs. But there was a limit. No man could be levered too far out of the pattern.

And now poor Paul had been softened and he was all pliable and simply waiting for a new mold to form him again. Harland hoped that this time he would be able to do a better job of shaping his son. He was going to take Paul back home with him and they would have a fine life together. They would hunt and fish and go to baseball games and there would be nothing to trouble them.

But Harland was troubled now.

He was pacing the room, jumpy as a cat and, although the room was not hot, he was sweating. He knew what the matter was. It was the same way he'd felt when he first arrived—when he'd put off phoning Paul that first night. Now he intended to ask Paul to come home and things like that always made him nervous. That was all it was—what else could it be?

He needed a drink.

He would have a drink, two at the most, then he would be calm and he could put the question to his son.

"Paul?" he said, softly.

Paul was asleep. Harland would not disturb him. The sleep would do him good. Harland leaned over the bed and smiled; then he moved toward the door but, with his hand on the doorknob, he hesitated. He ran his tongue across his lower lip. Then he went back to the closet and opened the door. His clothing was arranged neatly on the bar. Paul had no clothing; he refused to allow Harland to fetch his things from the apartment. Harland looked at Paul, then looked into the closet. He seemed to be pondering some crucial consideration, as if wondering if he should throw a coat over the sleeping boy, perhaps. He was sweating more now. After awhile he knelt down and reached into the back of the closet. His shoulders shifted and something crackled. He was leaning right in under the clothing now and he seemed to be breathing hard. . .or sighing. He stood up and closed the closet door. Paul slept on. Harland looked puzzled.

Chapter Fifty-One

They were going to be late.

LaRoche was ready to go but Stella, who was never on time, was taking particular care as she dressed, humming happily to herself. She was overjoyed. They had started up the social ladder now, going right up hand over fist. Stella had never even met the Superintendent; now they had been invited to his home. The Superintendent! He almost wasn't a cop at all. Now she was fluttering around the bedroom, looking in her jewel box, opening dresser drawers.

"Oh, bother!" she muttered.

LaRoche stood in the doorway. He wore a dark suit and tie; the toes of his shoes gleamed.

"Almost ready, dear?"

"Have you seen my new earrings, darling?"

LaRoche didn't answer. He looked at his wristwatch as if it were a witness.

"I can't seem to find them. . ."

"You'll have to hurry, Stella."

"Yes. But where can they have got to? I'm so scatterbrained. Let me think. . ."

"We're late," he said patiently.

Stella giggled. She had girlish mannerisms like that; they were sexy. She said, "When a woman loses her earrings, it's usually in some man's bed. . ." LaRoche and Stella had no problems of that sort. She could joke about it. "Not me! I can lose them in my own bedroom. . ."

"Darling. . ."

"Oh, well. I can wear the jade ones, I suppose.

199

Maybe the new ones were too big, anyway.''

"Stella. . ."

"Oh, all right. I'm coming. But I should think that you ought to be able to find them, darling. You find murderers and all, can't you detect my earrings?'' Now that they were socializing with the Superintendent she had finally admitted that her husband was a cop. She laughed. "There must be a clue," she said, thinking of LaRoche in a deerstalker hat, peering through a magnifying glass as he sought evidence of the missing jewelry.

LaRoche sighed. He looked at his watch.

Chapter Fifty-Two

Rosy Winters sat at the formica bar in the Jamaica and toyed with her usual rye and coke. She didn't much like rye and coke but she didn't know what else to order and she had to drink something while she looked over the prospective clients. She was chewing gum, levering it around with her tongue for awhile and then suddenly chomping on it, like a cat playing with a mouse. Rosy was eighteen years old and she had only been a whore for a few months and was still learning her trade. She was confident that she would be a good whore once she had a bit more experience, because she liked her work and she worked hard at it. Rosy had come down from Thunder Bay to seek her fortune and wrote her proud parents that she was a receptionist in a hotel, which was sort of true—she did receive men in hotels. Now she was looking for a man but it was a slow night. The only potential customer was a fat guy at the bar and he was awful; he had no teeth and he slurped his beer like a whale straining in plankton.

Rosy watched him for awhile, thinking that she wouldn't turn him down if he approached her but that, ugly as he was, she wasn't going to make the first move.

Then she watched the go-go dancers reflected in the mirrors up and down the back of the room. They were just as bad as she was, Rosy figured. They sold their bodies and she sold hers and just because guys only looked at them didn't make it any different. Worse, maybe. They were like cock-teasers, that was it, while Rosy gave value for money.

She sipped rye and coke. She chewed her gum. She looked at the fat man again. Another young woman came in and took a seat at the bar. She was dressed sexily and Rosy felt annoyed. With all these amateurs around it was hard for a professional to ply her trade and it wasn't so easy to differentiate between a liberated woman and a whore. It was sort of an identity crisis, she figured. She looked speculatively at the woman. The woman was looking at the fat man. The fat man addressed only his beer. Good luck to her, Rosy thought.

Presently, Rosy had to go to the woman's room.

On Sundays in Canada one has to buy food in order to get a drink and the garbage cans outside the toilets were overflowing with curling cheese sandwiches which had been sold and resold week by week but never eaten and had finally been discarded that week when they became too disreputable to sell again, even to thirsty Canadians.

Rosy came stepping through those sandwiches where they had spilled out on the floor like a deck of crusty cards dropped by an awkward shuffler. She stepped daintly. The woman's room was on one side of the row of trash cans, the men's room on the other. Beyond the woman's room there was another door that opened out on the alley, where the trash cans would presently be placed. This door was habitually kept barred so that no one could use the toilets without passing through the bar and, unless they were shameless, buying a drink. But the bar had been lifted now. Rosy did not notice this. Why should she?

She went into the woman's room and did not bother to lock the door behind her. She was not overly modest. She sat down and looked at the writing on the walls. She always read the graffiti to see if there was anything new, but there never was, although some of the remarks had been repeated since her last visit. Rosy wished that she were clever enough to write something original on the toilet wall but the only thing she could ever think of to write was "fuck."

She chewed her gum and read the walls and when the door opened she looked up, expecting it to be one of the go-go dancers.

When she saw it was a man, she was annoyed.

She said, "Hey! You're in the wrong room, Buster!"

Then she saw his face.

Rosy's head tilted up as she watched him come, her face going up inch by inch. She had started chewing her gum very fast all of a sudden. He leaned over her. Her jaws were working and his jaws were working, too. She was chewing right in his face with her eyes wide and his face came down.

Rosy screamed once.

Chapter Fifty-Three

It was the best assignment she had ever had, she thought. Her name was Anna Jennings and she was a policewoman and now she was dressed like a hippie girl and prowling the bars and enjoying it tremendously. If she hadn't decided to be a cop she probably would have been a hippie, she thought; maybe a whore; even, although not if all the customers looked like that fat guy slurping his beer. She wondered if he might be the killer. He was ugly enough to be a killer, although probably not as ugly as a werewolf. She had heard the werewolf talk but it didn't bother her.

She had a gun.

Now she had a drink, too, and she was thinking that anyone could be the killer. There was no way to tell until he started killing. Maybe it was one of those bearded kids with long hair; they could pass for werewolves on a dark night, no doubt about it. That was one of the big drawbacks in being a hippie girl—you had to consort with hippie guys.

She sipped her drink.

Maybe she would have been a go-go dancer, she thought. There were plenty of things to be, if one wasn't a cop. She was pretty enough. No one had tried to pick her up yet, though. But she figured that someone would, pretty as she was. it might be fun. She'd have to go with him, because it was her job, and it might be interesting finding out if he wanted to kill her or screw her. None of the victims had been raped so she didn't think there would be anything equivocal about his approach. And she was getting paid for it, with expenses, too. It was certainly a fine assignment.

Then she heard Rosy scream.

Anna was a good cop, despite her speculations about being other things, and she had her gun out and was speaking into her radio even as she went down the iron staircase to the basement. She stopped at the foot of the stairs, beside the trash-cans.

The door to the woman's room was swinging and it had been a woman's scream.

Anna held her gun in both hands and got it well out in front of her, pointed at the door. She had never shot anyone but her hands were steady and she wasn't worried about that. Still, she hesitated for a moment—there was something eerie about the way the door swung in and out.

"Police!" she called. "Come on out of there!"

The door swung more slowly.

Anna could hear sounds behind the door—heavy panting, the rustle of movement—and then the sounds ceased and there was a silence so profound that it seemed like noise itself.

"Out!" she cried.

She had begun to shake.

"Come out with your hands up! Now!"

Her voice sounded all right, she thought; it was authoritative and confident. She hoped it worked.

She hoped he would come out because she didn't want to have to go in after him—but she didn't want to wait for help, either, because the girl might still be alive in there. She should have been a go-go dancer, she thought. The door had stopped swinging.

Anna took one step forwards, following the gun.

Then the door burst open and he came out fast and right at her. His head was down and his shoulders looked as wide as an axe handle. He was coming quickly, but time seemed to falter in her mind, so that she saw him coming in slow motion.

She pulled the trigger.

The gun bucked in her hands and the sound bounced off the walls. She saw the bullet hit him on the shoulder. A furrow indented his coat and shreds of material jerked up. But he didn't stop; he didn't even hesitate. He loomed up before her and his arm came around in a savage backhand swipe. It was still slow motion in her awareness; she saw that thick arm come around like the boom of a ship and she was trying to fire the gun again and then her head was going around to the side as his forearm struck her. Her neck seemed to rotate with terrible, inexorable slowness. Her face turned from him and she was looking at the wall and her head went on around and she was looking at the stairs behind her and as she saw them she knew that her head should not be able to turn all the way around on her torso and then the sound of her neck as it broke was as loud as the gunshop bouncing off the walls.

A pair of uniformed cops named Dougherty and

Clancy were patrolling Yonge Street and had stopped in front of the Jamaica. There were billboards on either side of the entrance with photographs of some of the go-go girls and the two cops were admiring the pictures and listening to the music from within. Dougherty had tipped his red-banded hat back and Clancy had pulled his brim down and tilted his head back.

When they heard the shot, they turned their faces and looked at each other.

The shot seemed to have come from the alley beside the bar. Dougherty pulled his hat back down and they moved into the alley. The alley was empty. It was a narrow passage with brick walls on both sides and a wooden fence at the rear. The two cops went down side by side, completely blocking it. They could still hear the music from the Jamaica; it came out distorted through the fabric of the wall, the sounds dragged out into an eerie, pulsating dirge.

They paused halfway down.

They looked at each other and Clancy shrugged. Dougherty nodded at the door that opened into the basement. They moved on to it and Clancy reached for the handle just as the door slammed out. It was a heavy, metal door and it came out hard. It broke his hand in four places and his elbow jumped out of its socket.

Clancy screamed with pain.

The man came out as if he had sprung from the bowels of the earth. His arms were out and up. Both cops grabbed him and he grabbed both of them, one in each hand.

His big torso leaned to the side and he threw Dougherty away like a stone. Dougherty was a stout man, tall and broad; he turned over once in the air, his legs scissoring, and he came down backwards on the top of the fence and his body closed up like a jackknife.

He made no sound.

Clancy was shouting, trying to grapple with one hand, the other shattered. He held the man by the shoulder. It was like grasping a lump of iron. The man turned him with one hand and his other hand moved up, the fingers clawed. His hand went to Clancy's throat, moving almost gently, caressing the soft flesh. He felt around where the big artery was pulsing. Then his hand turned, digging in with the steady rotation of a corkscrew.

Clancy's mouth was open but he could no longer shout.

A line of red opened along his throat, as straight and as bright as the red band on his hat. Then it flowed out of shape. Like a scarlet shadow, it washed over his shoulders. . .

Chapter Fifty-Four

Superintendent Bruno Langford was a big, bluff fellow who favored a gentleman farmer in a milder land. He pressed a Scotch on LaRoche and clapped him heartily on the back. LaRoche thought maybe it wouldn't be so bad, after all. Langford's wife was a fashionably self-possessed woman, slender and aristocraftic; she took Stella aside and said, "You must call me Margot, dear," and then winced when Stella did. She impressed Stella greatly. The house impressed her, as well. There were oil paintings on the walls and the table was set with silver and candelabra, gleaming through the open oak doors. The silver reminded Stella of her missing earrings, but she was in far too happy a mood to feel depressed about that. She looked at the paintings, which were modern and formless.

Margot Langford waved a languid hand.

"My soul feasts on art, don't you know," she said.

The paintings looked like oil spills to Stella, who nodded and said, "Quite so."

The Superintendent winked at LaRoche, then rolled his eyes, and LaRoche grinned. Maybe not so bad.

As they started in to the dining room, Margot said, "Now, no nasty shop talk at the table, Bruno."

Then the phone rang.

Public relations had to wait, Langford saw that as he came back into the room, looking sick.

LaRoche raised his eyebrows.

"Not at the table, remember," Margot said.

"Why don't you shut up," said Langford.

She turned crimson.

"Another one?" LaRoche said.

"Worse," said Langford.

LaRoche got up and followed the Superintendent to the telephone. He listened.

"Oh my God," he said.

The dinner was aborted and Stella sat there at the table, distraught and miserable and confused.

Margot, insulted in front of guests—low born, common guests, true, but still guests—had stormed off to her bedroom. Langford was on the phone and LaRoche had left. He hadn't even said goodbye; he seemed to have forgot she was there. Now she didn't know what to do. She had lost her appetite, but that didn't matter for she could hardly sit there alone, serving herself from silver bowls and pouring wine from decanters. She could hear the Superintendent's voice as he spoke excitely into the telephone. He had forgot her, too. She wondered if she should ask him to call her a taxi or just sit there until someone remembered her. She knew there would be no socializing now. The rungs of the social ladder had been broken as if by sympathetic vibration with the neck of Anna Jennings and the back of Officer Dougherty.

Stella wished that Steve would hurry up and catch that horrid killer. . . .

Chapter Fifty-Five

LaRoche came into the office, his sweating brow as shiny as the toes of his dress shoes and his scowl as black. Greene was already there, looking stunned.

"Are they. . .?"

Greene nodded, then shook his head from side to side, the double gesture strangely awkward.

"Dougherty is alive. . .barely," he said. "His

back is broke. He may make it, Steve. The doctor says there's a good chance he can make it. He was. . .hell, he was thrown up in the air and came down on the top of a fence. Just thrown up in the air, Steve. My God, the strength he must have. . ."

"The other two?"

"They're both dead," Greene said, softly.

"Oh, Christ!"

Greene lowered his head into his hands.

"Jennings' neck was snapped," he said. "By a blow, it seems. She was lying in a pile of cheese sandwiches, Steve. Goddamn cheese sandwiches. That seemed to make it worse, somehow, those sandwiches. It just doesn't seem right. . .like a pratfall, you know? Like it was slapstick. Clancy. . .he bled to death before anyone got to him. His throat was open like a tin of sardines. You could see the sinew and stuff in his neck, the flesh was rolled open like a tin can, sinew and stuff. . .like sardines. . ."

"Snap out of it!" LaRoche shouted.

Greene flinched. His eyes were watery.

He said, "Yeah."

Then he said, "Okay, I've been objective, Steve. I didn't think about it until you asked. One thing. We think Jennings got a slug into him."

LaRoche's eyebrows went up.

"She fired once and there was plenty of blood in the basement. We found the slug so maybe she just winged him or maybe it went right through him. We think the blood was his. Jennings didn't bleed at all. There was blood all over the toilet. . .from the other girl. . .but we think the blood in the basement is his." He paused. "There's blood in the alley, too, but that might all be from Clancy. The

210

lab boys are working on that now."

"If she did. . .can Dougherty speak?"

"Not now. He was conscious for awhile. . .he didn't make much sense. He just seemed surprised at the way he'd been thrown right up in the air. He's a big guy."

"Did he say if this. . .what the killer looked like?"

Greene shook his head.

"He's got a chance," he said.

"Who was the girl?"

"Rosy Winters. Prostitute. Young and pretty. Got parents living." Greene sighed.

"Yeah. Well, if he's wounded, if Anna got a bullet into the bastard. . ."

"He'll have to hole up somewhere," Greene said, nodding. "I was thinking about that. I figure he'll go to ground somewhere close by."

"If he's hit hard enough. . ."

"I don't mean that. If this guy doesn't look human. . .normal, I mean. . .if he can't pass as a normal man, especially if he's got a gunshot wound in him. . .Well, I figure that a search of the area, empty buildings, basements, lofts. . .we just might turn him up. And there's this, Steve. . .except for the girl behind the stadium, the murders have all taken place within a small area. The stadium is off-set but. . .well, look here. . ."

LaRoche came around to look over Greene's shoulder. Greene had a street map spread out on the desk and he'd marked it in red pencil, with straight lines connecting crosses.

Greene said, "If we concede that James. . . the guy from the King Eddie. . .if we grant that James did see the killer lurking by the hotel, then it forms an almost perfect triangle. See? With the hotel at one angle and the tenement where the Carlyle girl lived at the opposite angle, then the Eton Center is the apex, it closes the wedge here and. . .''

"Oh, for crissake, Joe," LaRoche snorted.

Greene looked up, puzzled.

"Do you imagine this son-of-a-bitch got a compass or a protractor out and figured a geometric design beforehand? That's crap, Joe."

Greene looked hurt and LaRoche was sorry he'd snapped at him. Greene had been trying to see it objectively. Now, defensively, he said, "Well, no. . .I didn't think that. . .I just meant that we ought to search the area enclosed by the triangle, not that he planned it that way. He might have a hideout nearby, is the thing." Greene's shoulders shifted around and he flushed. "If he can't just walk down the street like you or I. . .well, it was a thought. The Jamaica Tavern is right in the center of the triangle," he added, determined to complete it.

"Wait a minute!" LaRoche said. "That's something. Wasn't the Carlyle girl drinking in the Jamaica just before she was killed?"

"Yeah, we established that, Steve; I was coming to that."

"Well, why in hell didn't you say so, instead of playing Pythagoras with that triangle stuff?"

"You didn't give me a chance to. . .''

"So there's a pretty good chance that the killer drinks in the Jamaica," LaRoche was saying.

"Maybe. Or lurks around there."

"If the same guy was in there both nights. . .''

"He wasn't in there tonight, thought," Greene said.

"How do you know that?"

"I checked it out, Steve. The only guy that was in there all night was still at the bar when they heard the girl scream. The killer came in from the alley."

"Damn!"

"But listen. . .the basement door is always kept locked. It's got a bar on the inside. So someone was there earlier and lifted the bar, Steve. . ."

"Jesus. It was premeditated; if he had to unlock the door hours before, then the bastard was planning to kill someone there all along. . .it wasn't a sudden rage, an impulse that sprang up from opportunity. That might make it easier for us, Joe. . .if he's planning these things, then maybe we can out-think him, predict his next. . .but, hell. . .it's more sickening, too. . ."

"They had quite a few customers in there earlier," Greene said. "Mostly businessmen, looking at the girls on their lunch hour. Regulars. A few strangers, though. I got descriptions of them."

"Good. Anything?"

"Nothing that fits in with what Pearsall or Clanton saw. . .or the other one. . ."

LaRoche was stroking his chin.

He said, "I think we may have something there. The killer might be a regular there or it might be the other way around. . .maybe all the girls were regulars. It could be the link we've been looking for. That's a rough place. . .some madman who gets his kicks killing girls he considers depraved. . .planning it ahead of time. . ."

"I don't know, Steve. . .Dawson wasn't old enough to drink legally. Drummond was certainly too young."

"Yeah. Still, I think we're on to something, I feel it. The Carlyle girl. . .do we know if she was a regular?"

"It might be in the report; it didn't seem important at the time. Easy enough to find out."

"And the. . .this girl tonight?"

"Rosy Winters. Yeah, she was in there every-night. Working, I guess, although the bartender wouldn't admit that."

Greene had the Carlyle report out, relieved to be doing something, to have some lead no matter how slender. He was running his index finger down the page.

"Doesn't say," he said.

"Check it out with the bartender. She lived with a man, didn't she? If the bartender doesn't remember, check with him. . .but try the bartender first; I guess the boyfriend won't want to think about it.

"That's right," Greene said. "An American kid. He might have moved out, though. He isn't a suspect. I don't suppose he'll want to go on living there. . .it can't be much fun walking up and down those stairs, where his girl was killed. Poor kid was home when it happened, too. Let's see . . . here we are. . .James. . .Paul James. . .he's from. . ."

"James?"

"Paul James. He. . ."

LaRoche's face had gone hard as flint.

"And that fruitcake from the King Edward?"

Greene blinked.

"Harland James," he said.

They looked at each other for a few moments.

LaRoche said, "It's a common enough name. But. . .that guy was a Yank, too, wasn't he?"

"Christ, Steve. . .do you think. . .?"

"Something," said LaRoche.

"If it is him. . .if we had him right here in this office. . .But why would he. . .?"

LaRoche had moved away from the desk; he was thinking, gazing at the wall. He said, "You know, if a man wanted to kill someone. . .and he thought to throw a smokescreen out, to confuse the issue. . .if he were to kill a couple other people, first. . .people of the same type, in the same circumstances. . .and then if he got the idea that he might get us on a false scent with that animal crap. . .get us looking for a werewolf, for crissake. . .Well, it's ridiculous, but if the guy was crazy enough to kill the way he does, who knows how his mind might work?"

"So maybe he wanted to kill his son's girlfriend. . .there could be motive there, Steve; the Carlyle girl wasn't as good as she might have been. . ."

LaRoche pounded his fist into his palm.

"Ah, hell. . .it's no good," he said.

"It makes sense. . ."

"Naw. I was getting carried away, Joe. It would have made sense. . .but why would he kill again, tonight, after the Carlyle girl was already dead?"

Greene looked at the wall.

"Maybe he just got in the habit, Steve," he said.

LaRoche jerked his face around. He thought that Greene was joking and he didn't like it. But then he saw that Greene was dead serious—and he understood it.

"Jesus," he said. "That's terrible!"

Greene was nodding.

"Maybe you'd better have another talk with Harland James, Joe, Now."

"Shall I bring him in?"

"You might. Yeah, I think so."

"Warrant?"

"We've got dead people, Joe. We got dead girls and we got dead cops; you got a gun, you don't need a warrant at all."

Chapter Fifty-Six

He was human again.

He could think now but his thoughts were muddled and confused and there was a fiery pain in his shoulder. He was sitting in his car but he didn't remember getting there. He remembered leaving the hotel, he'd gone out for a drink, but he hadn't had one. What had happened—well, he knew what had happened, but he recalled it in a strange way, in the third person, as if he had witnessed it but not been involved in it.

Maybe that was true.

Maybe—at those times—he was really not himself; maybe his own mind left his body—left what his body became—and hovered in the air above, observing, drifting away from his physical self like a soul from a corpse.

He had killed again.

He knew that. He could still taste the blood in his mouth. It had tasted, he knew, wonderful then. . .hot and thick and wonderful in the mouth of that other thing. But it tasted terrible now, metallic and bitter.

But why had he killed again?

He knew that he'd had a reason for killing the first two girls but now he couldn't remember what that reason had been. Had he been laying a false scent? Or just. . .practicing? He didn't know. He knew why he'd had to kill the third girl, though; he was glad he could remember that. It soothed his remorse and shrouded his guilt. But those feelings were still there, submerged, floating like some bloated creature waiting to surface.

He wished he could brush his teeth.

Everything was all mixed up in his human mind now and he was hurt and bleeding and he didn't know what to do. He couldn't go back to the hotel like he was. The police would be sure to get him and they wouldn't understand—how could they, now that he did not understand himself?

He slumped behind the wheel, holding his torn shoulder. A drumbeat throbbed at his temples but the blood no longer pulsed from his wound. He tried to reason.

Well, there was one place he could go.

Come to me, she had told him. If it happens again, come to me. He had not thought he would ever go to her again. She hadn't helped him at all. But she was not his enemy and he had to go somewhere and maybe, this time, she would tell him. . .what he was.

He started the car.

He was human; he could drive.

He could drive directly to her, too, for he had always been able to follow a trail.

He had instincts.

Chapter Fifty-Seven

Paul remembered her in vignettes, in snatches, in solid lumps of unconnected images and echoes; he turned the memories over in his mind like the leaves of a book, thumbing past some, lingering here and there, passing on to a new page that had no relation to the one before. He remembered her in moods, loving, angry, scornful, indignant, playful, in turn, with the emotion in full bloom and no transition between. Once she had been going on at him about how wicked it was that women tennis players were not paid as much as the men. Paul had no firm convictions on the flagitiousness of that injustice—in fact, he had not even known it was so—but Sarah had ranted on and on and finally he had said, "Don't worry, Sarah; when they hold the dishwashing championship of the world at Wimbledon, it will all even out." He had anticipated absolute foaming at the mouth rage; instead she laughed with delight. She was not to be predicted. He was remembering that occasion now, stretched out on the bed in the hotel room, when the knock sounded on the door.

It was just like a re-run.

One cop had a uniform with a red band on his hat and the other cop was in mufti and Paul thought for a moment that time had reversed itself just as it did in his memories and that they had come to tell him that Sarah was dead all over again. He stepped back from the door; he walked backwards in his own footsteps, reversing time like a film, as if he could thereby negate it. But the cops did not follow suit. They didn't backstep away from the door; they walked into the room.

"Who are you?" Greene said.

Both cops were looking around, not at Paul.

"What? I don't. . ."

"Is Mr. James here?"

"I'm James."

Greene looked at Paul then.

"No you're not," he said simply.

Paul blinked. Then he dawned on him and he said, "Oh! You mean my father. . .it's his room. . ."

"Harland James."

"Yes, my father. . ."

"Then you're Paul James?"

Paul nodded, slowly. He felt confused, brought back from memory to reality too quickly.

"Yes. I'm the one you want, if it's something about Sarah. . ." He paused. He couldn't remember her last name. It amazed him. Then he remembered. "Sarah Carlyle," he said. He had remembered by recalling her father's name; the name seemed to have no relation to the girl in any way, and that was remarkable for she had always insisted on using it; she had refused to use Paul's name, to pretend that they were married. Maybe it wasn't so remarkable, after all.

"Where is your father?" Greene said.

"Why. . .I don't know. I was asleep. He was

here. He must have gone out. But what's this about?''

The uniformed cop was still looking around the room, as if Harland James might suddenly spring into sight, standing just behind Greene and moving his head; Greene looked steadily at Paul now. He seemed to be having trouble deciding what to say.

He said, "Mind if we have a look around?''

"Well. . .no. . .but I don't. . .''

The uniformed cop moved past Paul.

"Listen, why. . .?''

"We'd like to ask your father a few further questions,'' Greene told him.

"I didn't know you'd asked him any.''

"About the. . .the thing he thought he saw.'' Greene watched Paul sharply.

"Oh, you've got it wrong. My father didn't see anything. He was there, earlier, but he'd already left when. . .''

"He hasn't told you?''

Paul's mouth opened. His mind had begun to spin around like a carousel. Greene could almost see his mind revolve. Greene knew the boy was innocent. Now he felt pretty sure that the father wasn't. He spoke slowly; Paul had lost his girl, that was bad enough. . .now. . .Greene said, "Harland James reported seeing what might have been the killer. . .this was not the night that your girl was killed, it was two nights before.''

Paul felt as if his head was wobbling.

He said, "But, that's impossible. . .he never mentioned it to me. . .if he'd seen Sarah's murderer, he might have wanted to protect my feelings, but before she was. . .why wouldn't he have told me if he saw something?''

"Why, indeed?"

Paul's lips moved but no sound came out. The uniformed cop was moving around the room. He ducked down quickly to look under the bed. He always felt foolish looking under a bed but you had to; people really did hide under beds. He moved to the closet and opened it and began to inspect the clothing that hung there. Greene didn't want to face Paul any longer. He walked over to the dresser and started opening drawers. Paul stood still but his mind was moving. Little bristles started to ripple at the back of his mind and the hairs stood up stiff on the back of his neck. His father had always been strange. Like a manic-depressive, he seemed to go through periods of deep gloom and terrible restlessness. But he was always able to come out of it, to cure himself. He never went to a doctor or took drugs. He would go off alone on a hunting trip, he would be gone for a week or so and when he returned he was calm and content. It as just that the demands of society got to him, that was all; surely that was all. A few days of solitude in the wilderness were all he needed, just a vacation away from the rat race. . . .

"Nothing on the clothes."

Paul heard the uniformed cop speak from the closet. What could be on the clothes?

"Check his shoes," Greene said.

The cop hunkered down.

"Some mud," he said. The word itself was a verbal shrug. They had four young girls dead. . . they had two cops dead and one maybe dying. He was looking for more than mud.

Greene shut a drawer. He moved away from the dresser.

The uniformed cop said, "Nothing." Then he said, "Here's a shoe box, I think; it's wrapped up in plastic. . ."

Greene moved towards the closet.

Paul could hear plastic rustle and crackle. He found himself moving across the room. The cop was kneeling, Green was leaning over his shoulder and Paul came up to stand behind Greene. It occurred to him that he might have asked them for a search warrant. But you didn't think about things like that if you weren't a criminal.

The plastic was unwrapped and it was a shoe box.

"Jeez. . .it stinks," the cop said.

He glanced up at Greene, his face wrinkled.

"Open it," said Greene.

The cop took the lid off the box.

And the three of them looked at the rotting head of a wolf. . . .

Chapter Fifty-Eight

The wolf's head had been torn from the neck and it was soft with corruption. The uniformed cop gagged. He put the lid back on the box and looked up at Greene.

"Well, that's the answer," Greene said. "We know who did it and we know how he did it. Now all we have to do is find the bastard."

And Paul knew something else.

He knew it with a sudden certainty, without any doubt at all—had he known it all along, in some dark unconscious depths where it could lurk without recognition?

"Oh my God!" he said. "My mother!"

Greene looked at him, startled.

Paul stared right through him.

Greene said, "Your father. . . ." Paul said, "My mother. . ."

Greene shook his head. Well, the kid was in shock; it was understandable. He went over to the telephone.

He called LaRoche.

"Steve? It's him, all right."

Greene was watching Paul as he spoke into the phone. The uniformed cop was holding the shoebox and Paul was staring at the box and the cop was staring at him, as if he expected the boy to make a sudden grab for the box.

Greene said, "No, he isn't here. But we found. . .Steve, he's got the head of a wolf here. In a box. Had it wrapped up in plastic. No, just the head. . .a wolf's head. . .all rotten. So that's it." He listened, still watching Paul.

"Yeah, his son is here. What? No, he doesn't know anything about it."

Greene's eyes flicked over Paul. He felt very sorry for the kid.

"The kid is in shock, Steve," he said. "He's gone over the edge. He thinks his mother did it. . ."

So that was it.

But it wasn't. Steve LaRoche knew that it wasn't. LaRoche was the skeptic and Greene had been willing to believe anything, and now Greene said, "So that's it."

But it wasn't.

The pathologist always looked a bit timid and nervous, with his tiny little mustache and his little fluttering hands, but now he looked nervous in a deeper way.

He was saying, "I haven't finished with the blood yet but. . ."

"I want to ask you something," LaRoche said.

". . .but it appears that—like the saliva—it's not completely human. . ."

"If," said LaRoche, and paused.

The pathologist looked attentive.

"If a man had a dead wolf. . .the head of a wolf. . .would it be possible to. . ." Christ, how did you say a thing like this? "Could he have chewed those girl himself and then poured or rubbed saliva from a dead wolf into the wounds?"

"A dead wolf?"

"That's what I said."

"You mean. . .freshly killed?"

"No, I don't mean that."

"But that is the point. . ."

"Dead. Rotting."

"Oh," said the pathologist and he thought for awhile, but LaRoche knew that he wasn't contemplating the answer to LaRoche's question. He knew that. After awhile, he said, "Saliva. . .and blood. . .are organic, of course. If the wolf were dead, they would commence to corrupt. The saliva of a dead wolf would be necrotic, Steve. That was not the case."

LaRoche sighed. He had known that; he had asked, but he had known the answer all along.

Now the pathologist's hands were fluttering spasmodically.

"There's something more, Steve," he said.

"I thought there might be."

The pathologist looked surprised.

"Tell me," LaRoche said.

"I've completed the further tests on the saliva. I think it will be the same with the blood, as well. Steve, it seems that it was not a case of finding two separate samples of saliva in the wounds. Naturally, my first thought was that. . .well, I was wrong, although justifiably. There was only one saliva sample, Steve. . .but the cellular structure of that saliva was modified, mutated. . .in the process of changing, that it. It was as if some catalyst had caused human saliva to become. . .Steve, you don't seem surprised. You do understand what I'm saying?"

"Yes. I understand it."

"You. . .expected it?"

"I don't know," LaRoche said.

"The blood. . .I think it will prove. . .I can't explain this. . ."

"Don't," said LaRoche. "Don't even try. I don't want you to say anything about this to anyone."

The pathologist looked relieved.

He couldn't have explained it at all.

There was no wolf.

LaRoche had known that all along. There was the head of a wolf and Greene was satisfied and the newspapers need never know about the saliva—and the blood—but LaRoche knew there was no answer within the realm of science nor within the scope of the human mind. And he knew it was better if a question that could not answered were never asked.

The killer had to die.

225

Harland James had to die and LaRoche had to kill him.

Cronski had seen that right away, he remembered. LaRoche had not been a believer then and now there were further questions he thought to ask her. He knew one way. He wondered if there might be others.

He stood at the window, looking out but seeing nothing. He was scared. He shook himself but he did not throw the fear away; it rattled around in his guts like splinters of ice. It melted and flowed in his blood, then it froze again on his bones. It struck him that he had never been truly frightened before and, thinking that, he realized a thing that had never really occurred to him before. He realized that he was a brave man.

But he had to do it and no one else could.

LaRoche went out to his car.

He sat behind the wheel for awhile, with the windows rolled up and the doors locked and his thoughts filling the car like a bowl full of jelly. He thought of the inhuman strength that had hoisted heavy Dougherty high in the air and snapped Jennings' neck like a matchstick and opened Clancy's throat like—Greene had said it—like a tin of sardines. He thought of blood that was not quite human and saliva that was not quite lupine.

There was no wolf.

But there was no man, either.

Before he started the car, LaRoche checked his revolver. He opened the cylinder and spun it and he made sure that there was a bullet in the chamber and that it was the right bullet. . . .

Chapter Fifty-Nine

When N. V. Cronski saw who was standing at her door, her flesh rippled and her blood rolled through her veins as if it bore lumps of stone in the stream. He was standing back from the stone arch of the doorway, in the shadows, but she knew who it was with an instinct as certain as his own.

She smiled, holding the door open.

"You know me?" he said.

"Of course. I'm glad you've come."

He hesitated for a moment, then moved into the house; in the hallway he looked at the stone walls, turning his big head from side to side. The light from the door at the end hit his spectacles; they flashed like a heliograph. Cronski had closed the door and stood with her back to it. She looked far more the predator than he did now.

"I will not harm you," he said.

"I know."

He smiled then. "You have not changed much," he said.

"I?" she said, surprised; then she realized he was merely being sociable, making a commonplace courtesy to a woman he had not seen in some years. It seemed absurd. Smiling, she said, "Oh, I do not change so very much. But you. . ."

Her eyes widened.

"But you are wounded!"

He tucked his chin into the hollow of his shoulder, looking at the gouge through coat and flesh.

"Let me help you," Cronski said.

"You will help me? You are willing. . .now. .. "

"Of course! Oh, yes. . .of course. . ."

"I. . .I have killed," he said.

"I know; it is nothing."

"Nothing?" he said. His head swayed; she could not tell if he were shaking his head in negation or swinging it arouind like a beast at bay. "I had a reason," he said. His voice caught; he seemed to be whining, pleading. "I had a reason to kill someone. . .but there were others. . ."

Cronski was furious.

He should have been magnificent—he was whining.

She said, "And still you rationalize, you fool!"

He flinched back from the venom in her voice.

"You justify yourself. . .you say you had reason to kill. . .don't you understand? Do you fail to understand, even now? You kill because it is your nature!"

She looked closely to gauge his reaction.

"Perhaps," he said.

Cronski smiled. That was a start, a beginning.

"Come," she said. "Let me tend to your wounds."

She took him by the hand. He was submissive and docile; she was thrilled. She led him down the stone hallway to the big room of uncertain shadows and placed him in a chair by the fireplace. He sat very still. She removed his coat and shirt. The material stuck to the wound and she eased it away. The bullet had plucked a lump of flesh and muscle from the trapezius muscle just where it folded over his shoulder into his pectoral and when the slug plowed through blood had blossomed out—but already the wound had started to close

228

and heal!

Cronski's eyes gleamed as she saw this proof of his power.

She began to cleanse the wound but it was hardly necessary—she did it to demonstrate that she was his ally—his only friend in an alien world.

"Are you able to change at will, now?" she asked.

"I. . .don't know. No, not at will—against my will. I have changed involuntarily and without cause, without reason."

"Reason enough," she whispered. "To change—that is reason enough to change. But something has happened to you. You were not this way, before."

He nodded slowly. Cronski stepped back. He closed his shirt, as if with modesty.

"I am different," he said. "There was a girl . . . a girl I had to kill. . .it was as it had been with my wife, just as it was then. . .but there were others; they are vague in my mind—for it was not my mind at the time."

"Ah, but it was," she said, with satisfaction. "You and what you become are one."

His eyeglasses had slipped down onto the bridge of his nose; his head was hanging. He looked pitiful and weak. Cronski grimaced with distaste.

"You must understand that. . .you must admit it to yourself. When you are changed, your mind works differently, of course, but it is still your mind. You are not possessed. You cannot deny it, nor hide from it. . .you must come to grips with it. I can help you."

He nodded, lifting his head but slightly.

"Tell me. . .everything."

229

"There was a wolf," he said.

"Ahhh," she sighed.

He said, "I was distraught. There had been a letter. I went into the wilderness, I hunted. I had no gun—but I hunted. It had worked in the past, had soothed the terrible urge that raged within me. To kill an animal was enough. But this time. . .I killed a wolf. It was vague, perhaps I was. . .not myself; with my hands, I killed a wolf. I had never killed a predator before. It had. . .an effect upon me." His head was lowered; his eyes slid up to glance at her, as if sliding in the lenses of his glasses. Cronski was leaning towards him, clinging to his words. "I took a part of the wolf away with me. . .I took the head of the wolf. . .I don't know why. . ." Now his head was down lower and his eyes moved from side to side. "I was compelled to, I don't know why, a symbol or. . .It was a thing I looked at when I felt the urge. . .it seemed to make it easier to change, to smooth the transition. . .I don't know. . ."

"I know," said Cronski.

Her face was fierce with joy.

He looked up and she looked away; she did not want to look into his weak face—his face as a man.

She said, "The impulse to change has always been with you. . .but your body did not have a pattern. When you killed your wife. . ." She shot him a glance; he took it without flinching, his huge eyes staring at her. "You changed, then, but the change was not complete. It was formless. You became something other than man, but it was an uncertain, unfinished thing. Now you have killed a wolf. You know the blood of the wolf, and the flesh. The tissue of the wolf has come into your body and now your body knows the structure of the wolf's cells. . .its chromosomes, its molecules, the very atoms of its life force. . .It has given your mind a template from which to stamp the change. Do you understand? A design.''

"Am I then. . .truly a werewolf, now?"

"I think. . .yes. A wolfman."

He shuddered.

He should have exalted in his power—instead, he shuddered. Cronski felt a great frustration. He was, perhaps, unique in the world and he should have been filled with jubilant pride, he should radiate ecstasy at the dark celebration of his mystery. Instead, he shuddered. She turned and paced away, then turned back; she stood so that an edge of shadow fell across the lower part of her face and her teeth gleamed from that shadow as she drew her lips back.

"Change for me!" she said.

He started.

"Will you change? I must see it, I must know. . ."

"No!" He shook his head. His eyeglasses had slipped down from before his eyes, but his eyes retained the magnification. They were big and they were yellow. "I will not change," he said. "That is not why I came to you. . ."

"But you will change," she said. Her words hissed at him. "You will change when you must; you will kill again. . .and again; I cannot help you not to kill but—I can help you when you have killed!"

He looked at her in horror. He stood up, with great effort, as if his body were too great a burden to lift.

"You should be examined by doctors, scientists,

perhaps—although I think not—psychologists. But that is not possible. They would not understand. They are fools. You are a fool. Only you and I believe in werewolves. . .and you must stay with me!"

"No," he said. He looked sad. He had a power for which she would have gladly sold her soul and he looked sad and Cronski was disgusted.

He said, "I'll go now."

He was slipping away from her. His eyes were diminishing and their color was dull.

"No!" She moved between him and the door. "They will find you; they will kill you."

"That might be just as well," he said.

"Or take you alive. . .as a man. Do you know how it will be? Do you know? Caged in a cell, unable to change when the urge is upon you, the fabric of your body boiling with the need, your brain melting, your power denied you. . ."

He took a step to the side, as if off-balance. "No," he said, mouthing the word silently.

"You fool!" Her head came out like a cobra, striking at him. "Fool, fool, fool!"

Her face was ferocious; her lips drooled. He took a step back from her and she advanced. She looked as if she might spring upon him, sinking her teeth into his flesh, trying to devour his power with his blood. He was afraid of her. He gestured helplessly, turning his forearms over and his palms upwards. . .those hands that could dismember a wolf, turning helplessly. . . .

And then he saw what she was doing.

She was trying to frighten him or enrage him, to fill him with some emotion that would bring the change.

She sickened him—as a man.

Again she said, "Fool."

The word echoed like a drum, startling him. She, too, looked startled. Then the echoe came again and it was not the echo of her voice—someone was banging on the door.

Her face shifted; she was no longer fierce.

The knocker struck again.

He looked around in a panic.

"Wait here," she said. "Whoever it is, I will send him away. . ."

Chapter Sixty

It was Steve LaRoche.

"I'm sorry to trouble you so late but. . ."

"Yes, you are, rather; I'm afraid I can't ask you in, Sergeant. I have a guest."

LaRoche nodded. He was surprised. He didn't see her as the sort to entertain a lover yet, from her attitude, he guessed that was what she was doing. He felt embarrassed.

"If you can give me two minutes. . .?"

Cronski looked pained.

"What is it?"

"A question. . .there have been more murders and. . ." He looked suggestively into the hallway; she did not offer to let him in. Standing there in the high arch of the doorway with his hat in his hand, feeling foolish, he said, "Just one thing then.

Perhaps I might see you tomorrow?" She showed no response. "For now. . .a wolfman. . ."

He saw her eyes ignite.

"You believe? Now you believe?"

Slowly, LaRoche nodded.

"Ahhh," she sighed.

"A wolfman. . .would he possess the cunning to lay a false trail?"

"I don't understand?"

"As a. . .wolf. . .would he be able to reason? To attempt to lay the blame on a. . .a real wolf? To cover his own tracks with the tracks of a wolf?"

"Has he done that?" she asked; she seemed astounded.

"I'm not sure. A man might plan to do that; could the wolfman carry out that plan? There was. . ."

Suddenly Cronski was laughing.

She laughed silently, more with her teeth and her lips and not at all with her eyes.

"How droll!" she said. "How ironic!"

"I don't. . ."

"You don't understand? No, I suppose not. But the absurdity of it. . .he must have tried so very very hard to deny what he was. . .don't you see? He, of all people! To lay the blame on a wolf. . .to lay a trail that could lead only back to him. A wolfman might lay a false trail by using. . .a gun, a weapon. . .he might try to blame it on a man. . .My God! Oh, the fool! Gifted as few men have ever been, he denies it!"

LaRoche was turning his hat in his hands, totally confused. She was still laughing silently—and bitterly, now. And then, slowly, a change came over her countenance. Her lips turned down and

234

her eyes were thoughtful.

She said, "But of course. . .what else? Self-preservation. . .that is the strongest catalyst of all. . .the greatest justification. . ." She turned her head; she looked down the long hallway. LaRoche could see the dark cords standing out in her neck.

She turned back to LaRoche.

A look of hideous cunning had come upon her.

"He is here," she said.

LaRoche stood very still.

His bones seemed to have fused. Cronski was peering into his face, her own face very close, looming out at him.

"Will you see him?" she asked.

Now LaRoche felt limp. His bones were melting. He still held his hat in both hands; he didn't know what to do with it. He put it back on his head. Cronski moved away and he followed her down the hallway.

He took his gun out.

She stepped into the big room and moved aside. LaRoche stood just inside the door. Harland James was beside the fireplace, looking wildly about for an exit. There was none. There was but one door and in that door stood Steve LaRoche.

LaRoche brought his gun up and aimed it at James and he was going to shoot. James started to move, perhaps he was raising his hands in surrender, but LaRoche was going to kill him, anyway. He had determined that; he had no choice. But he hesitated as his finger started to close on the trigger. It was the eyes that stopped him—those big, helpless, harmless eyes behind the thick glasses. James was terrified and LaRoche delayed for an instant.

Then Cronski grabbed his wrist.

She was amazingly strong; she forced his arm down and she was looking back over her shoulder.

"Change!" she cried.

LaRoche struggled with her, keeping his eyes on James. James seemed bewildered, still looking this way and that as if seeking a shadow in which he could hide.

"Change! You must change!" She was screaming as with agony. "He will kill you—as a man!"

The words registered on Harland James. His head came around and he looked at LaRoche and those eyes were different now. They were still huge, stil magnified—but they were glowing.

"Oh my God," LaRoche whimpered.

He had stopped struggling with Cronski. Her hand fell away from his arm and she stepped back. James needed no help now—for he was no longer James. LaRoche and Cronski stood side by side. They were both staring at Harland James.

And he was changing.

His shoulders rose and his head came down and his arms came out. Tendons like steel hawsers drew his hands into talons and his thighs were sinewed with iron. His face shifted. It seemed to blur and go out of focus for a moment; when it set the bones had moved beneath the skin and the skin had darkened and the thick bristles were sprouting around his mouth. His eyes were yellow and his teeth were long.

LaRoche's hand was shaking on the gun and the wolfman's eyes were shining as it came.

Cronski's face was savage with joy.

"Kill!" she screamed.

She spoke to the wolfman but the word bored into LaRoche's melting mind. LaRoche took one step backwards. He knew that he was babbling with terror. The wolfman crouched, panting, golden eyes fixed on LaRoche's bubbling throat.

LaRoche knew he was going to die.

He knew he could not kill this thing with a gun.

And then he remembered that he could.

The wolfman's thighs tensed to spring and LaRoche shot him through the heart.

Chapter Sixty-One

LaRoche was sick with shock and fear and horror.

He leaned back against the wall, his gun hanging down at his side. He had fired only once. Harland James was human again and he was dead. He lay on the floor, his back arched and his torso twisted to one side; his eyeglasses had fallen off and one thick lens had cracked. It glinted beside him. Cronski stood over the body. She was trembling. he had been mortal, after all, and now he was dead and lost to her forever. Her eyes turned; she looked back and forth between the dead man and the man who had killed him. That magnificent creature. . . that insignificant man. . .she began to sob convulsively.

She sank to her knees beside the body.

LaRoche saw her lower her face. He thought she was going to kiss the dead man.

Then he gagged.

Cronski had lowered her face to his breast,

where the blood was spreading out like a brilliant flower. LaRoche turned away. He was too weak to stop her; it was hard enough just to breath.

He could hear her lapping at the tainted blood.

LaRoche moved past her into the room.

His bullet had shot the creature through and through and he could see the erupted exit wound in the back. He looked quickly, then looked away. Cronski was still kneeling there, her face lowered. . .her mouth red.

LaRoche shuddered. He turned and looked at the walls. He saw the bright scar almost at once. It was on the gray stone directly behind where the wolfman had crouched. LaRoche walked over there. He still had his gun in his hand, hanging down. He looked at the mark on the wall and then he walked around with his head down. After awhile he stopped. He seemed to realize that he was still holding the gun. He put it in his pocket. He brought his hand out. He knelt down and then he stood up and he put his hand in his pocket again.

He went to the telephone.

Cronski said something. It was moist and muffled.

LaRoche looked at her.

Her face came up, twisted in disbelief and terrible with regret.

"I didn't think he would die," she whispered.

LaRoche said nothing.

His hand was in his pocket.

Chapter Sixty-Two

"Funny where that bullet got to," said Joe Greene.

"Does it matter?" LaRoche said.

"Naw. Just funny. Still, a room like that. . .hard to light it even with arc lights. I guess it must have rolled through a crack or lodged between the stones. Whatever. It did the job. I wish I'd been with you, Steve. That bastard. . ."

He paused. He had an idea that LaRoche didn't want him to say any more. But he had to.

"Cronski is right around the bend, Steve," he said. "We gonna charge her with anything?"

"No," LaRoche said quickly.

"She was harboring. . ."

"No," he said again.

"Yeah. Right. Think what the newspapers would make of it if she got a chance to give testimony at a trial, huh?" He laughed, not too happily. "Right around the bend, she is; she still claims that he was a wolfman." He shook his head. "Just goes to show what a deranged mind can imagine, eh?" He had a semi-sheepish attitude now.

He said, "I feel silly, myself. Some of the ideas I had before we found that wolfhead. Boy! A guy can sure get some crazy ideas!"

"We all make mistakes," LaRoche said.

"You didn't, Steve; it didn't fool you."

"No, it didn't fool me," said LaRoche, and he smiled tolerantly at his friend, who had learned that a man had to be objective and limit his imagination, and then he went on home to his wife, who had little imagination to limit.

Stella kissed him and praised him for solving the murders. She knew he was sure to get a promotion now. But she was still annoyed that she had somehow managed to misplace her new earrings.

"They were solid silver, you know," she said.

"I know," said Steve LaRoche.